As the moon-dust settles on the 48th anniversary of Apollo 11, information is now coming to light that throws into serious doubt the authenticity of the Apollo story. Was the Apollo 11 Moon landing faked? Why do so many people doubt that America succeeded in landing men on the Moon? Is it simply a matter of conspiracy theory or are there hard facts to support the claim that man has never stepped foot on the lunar surface? Was it one small step for man, or one leap of faith for mankind?

What other sinister forces might be involved in NASA's claim that they put two men down on the moon in 1969, and what might it have to do with 9/11? After reading this book you'll know.

I want to believe looks at the numerous inconsistencies in the official story, faith, why people believe what they believe, and examines evidence in the search for truth.

I Want to Believe
By Michael Sprankle

A lie can travel halfway round the world while the truth is putting on its shoes.

- This quote has been attributed to Mark Twain, but it did not originate with him.

Charles Haddon Spurgeon (1834-92) attributed it to an old proverb in a sermon delivered on Sunday morning, April 1, 1855.

Foreword   *The Blind Faith of Manifest Destiny*

"I Want to Believe" is the phrase on a poster in Agent Fox Mulder's cramped basement office in the *X Files* television series. Wanting to believe is Mulder's core vulnerability. And for Mulder, wanting to believe is different from blindly believing. He is still an FBI investigator, of course, always trying to examine the facts; even if he occasionally searches for facts to support his theories instead of theories to support the facts. He's a lot like me.

Back before I realized that monsters were real and the triumph of truth was an illusion, I filled myself with faith. These were the days before everything we heard was an opinion, not a fact. The days before everything we saw was a perspective, not the truth.   Trust is like a pencil eraser. It gets smaller and smaller with every mistake; and if you tell a lie once, all your truths become questionable.

Faith can be best described as the complete trust or confidence in someone or something. Blind faith can be defined as belief that is not BASED on reason or evidence.

Having been raised in the church, I was subjected to faith at a very early age. Some people unfairly criticize religion, saying that it's based on faith. This would imply that their own positions aren't. But faith doesn't belong solely to the domain of religion. Atheists have faith that there is no God. Agnostics have faith that God's existence can never be proven.

Christianity says that the universe, and everything in it, was created by God in six days. Atheism/secularism says that everything, including people, came into existence as a result of natural causes.

Why do different people believe in different concepts of reality? The Apostle Paul taught people that "faith is the assurance of things hoped for, the evidence of things not seen."

Religion has many faiths, but it's really not about the faiths, it's about the faithful. It's not about what any sacred books say or don't say; they say everything, from the very best to the very worst. It's about how those who hold such books sacred, actually use them.

Religion is like a fire. It can warm our homes and cook our food, or it can burn those same houses to the ground and take a great many of us with it.

Those who adhere to religious doctrine agree to give up all of their critical thinking skills the moment they climb aboard the Holy Wagon. It's not an option with religion, because you cannot accept religion as truth and still retain the courage to question it.

Like most people, from time to time I have questioned my faith. One of the biggest events that happened that caused me to question my faith was 9/11. I personally lost six friends in that tragedy. Did religion cause 9/11? Many people will say yes, religion drove those planes into the towers. There is a long history of hate and violence being done in the name of God, and failing to admit it means failing to fix it.

How does religion have anything to do with 9/11? Religion itself isn't the point. it's the mindset of religious people, who have allowed themselves to believe a doctrine which their subconscious mind tells them is ludicrous. Then again, maybe it was all just blow-back.

   The official version of 9/11 says that nineteen "Arab terrorists" planned, financed, and executed the most improbable event in American history, all by themselves. This is beyond ludicrous. People hiding in a cave did it? Who are perhaps the most ardent believers in Bush's official story of 9/11? Religious people, because they have been conditioned to believe the impossible, so long as an authority figure tells them it's true.

   Bush blamed, ... well, he blamed somebody, generally categorized as "the terrorists." Since then, Americans have given it no more thought. Bush said "the terrorists" did it, so that's all there is to it. The "evil doers" were responsible. If you disagree, you are accused of aiding "the terrorists" (a concept that defies all logic). You are also called a conspiracy theorist.

When a large majority of a population has already been dutifully programmed by religion, and thereby stripped of its ability to question and use critical thought, an event such as 9/11 is a godsend (no pun intended) to any powerful group that would use such an event to further its agenda.

Who profits from endless wars? The war in Afghanistan? Who profits from the war in Iraq? Who profits more than Israel if we topple Iraq, Afghanistan, Iran, Syria, etc.? And the question that precedes them all: who profits from 9/11 itself? These are questions that demand answers and accountability, but they are questions not being asked.

Religion set the stage for using 9/11 to further an agenda, and whomever organized 9/11 recognized that fact.

Brilliant in its depravity, this group of planners realized how easy it is to manipulate religious people who already willingly adhere to irrational and disproven beliefs. The brilliance was in using their own religious trinkets and icons in the charade. There should be an award given to whoever came up with the idea of wrapping Bush around a Bible to further the agenda.

Is religion to blame for 9/11? Without a doubt, no. Are the people who refuse to question 9/11 to blame for it? Absolutely, because people who refuse to question something, regardless of its glaring irrationality, encourage it to continue. They just blindly look away.

Nobody with critical thinking skills can possibly believe the official story of 9/11, especially with the mountain of contradictory evidence readily available to everyone. And that mountain keeps growing.

As a religious country, we have been raised to believe whatever comes out of the mouth of the guy up front in the church. He wears a fancy robe, sometimes with a pretty sash or a big hat, and he is obviously in charge of the church. He is the leader.

From childhood, we are conditioned to tremble at his voice. In such an environment, it doesn't take long to eventually erase any inclination to question the authority figure. Toss in a few even bigger authority figures, such as a Jesus, God, and some disciples, and how dare you question authority?

It's actually brilliant. My own opinion is that the Roman leader Constantine recognized the enormous potential for crowd control which is inherent in religion, and he utilized it to perfection. In those days, most of the population was uneducated beyond knowing not to defy the emperor. They would believe in anything.

I like to believe that science and religion are compatible. Science, like religion, rests on faith: faith in the accuracy of what we observe, in the laws of nature, or in the value of reason. Science is based on theory.

Such statements imply that science and religion are not that different because both seek the truth and use faith to find it. Indeed, science is often described as a *kind* of religion.

Scientists give no special credence or authority, except insofar as they present comprehensive theories, novel analysis, and verified truths. To a large degree, science is based on nature. The nature of a natural order of things.

The orderliness of nature—the set of so-called natural laws—is not an assumption but an *observation*. It is logically possible that the speed of light could vary from place to place, and while we'd have to adjust our theories to account for that, or dispense with certain theories altogether, it wouldn't be a disaster. Other natural laws, such as the relative masses of neutrons and protons, probably *can't* be violated in our universe. Then again, who knows. Science is based on the faith that it's good to know the truth.

    Once I pulled back the curtain to reveal the thousands of inconsistencies and holes in the official 9/11 story I began to wonder what other lies we may have been fed in the name of patriotism. What else is behind the curtain?

    It didn't take me long before I started to look at the first moon landing back in 1969.

I have authored and/or co-authored five fiction novels. I also have a degree in film, and I have directed and produced several short films. I like to believe that I have the knowledge and ability to create a story, script it out, and produce a film from that story. The story however, does not necessarily have to be true. If I am a good enough story teller, people will believe it... or at least accept it.

As a young boy, I enjoyed looking up at the night sky from our Pennsylvania home as much as the next guy. With much less light pollution than today, the stars were everywhere. But the stars I really had my eye on were the ones out in Hollywood. As soon as I had my high school degree in hand, I headed to Penn State University to study film making.

When I was thirteen, on July 20, 1969, my parents, my sister and I watched in awe as American astronauts Neil Armstrong and Edwin "Buzz" Aldrin became the first humans ever to land on the moon. About six-and-a-half hours later, Armstrong became the first person to walk on the moon. As he took his first step, Armstrong famously said, "That's one small step for man, one giant leap for mankind."

The Apollo 11 mission occurred eight years after President John Kennedy announced a national goal of landing a man on the moon by the end of the 1960s. Apollo 17, the final manned moon mission, took place in 1972.

During this period of history, the United States was involved in The Cold War with the Soviet Union. The Russians had more warheads, more soldiers and a more sophisticated space program. They were getting many firsts when it came to space exploration. By 1967, NASA was nowhere near living up to JFK's goal of landing a man on the moon by the end of the decade.

One of the biggest obstacles (and there were many others) that NASA encountered were the Van Allen radiation belts. These belts are the rings of charged particles held high above the Earth by its magnetic field. NASA had covertly tried sending a German shepherd through one of those belts. It didn't end well. The bite of the belts was worse than its bark.

The American effort to send astronauts to the moon had its origins in an appeal President John Kennedy made to a special joint session of Congress on May 25, 1961:

"I believe this nation should commit itself to achieving the goal, before this decade is out, of landing a man on the moon and returning him safely to Earth."

At the time, the United States was still trailing the Soviet Union in space developments, and Cold War-era America welcomed Kennedy's bold proposal.

In 1966, after five years of work by an international team of scientists and engineers, the National Aeronautics and Space Administration (NASA) conducted the first unmanned Apollo mission, testing the structural integrity of the proposed launch vehicle and spacecraft combination.

Then, on January 27, 1967, tragedy struck at Kennedy Space Center in Cape Canaveral, when a fire broke out during a manned launch-pad test of the Apollo spacecraft and Saturn rocket. Three astronauts were killed in the fire.

Despite the setback, NASA and its thousands of employees forged ahead, and in October 1968 Apollo 7, the first manned Apollo mission, orbited Earth and successfully tested many of the sophisticated systems needed to conduct a moon journey and landing. In December of the same year, Apollo 8 took three astronauts to the dark side of the moon and back, and in March 1969 Apollo 9 tested the lunar module for the first time while in Earth's orbit. That May, the three astronauts of Apollo 10 took the first complete Apollo spacecraft around the moon in a dry run for the scheduled July landing mission.

At 9:32 a.m. EDT on July 16, with myself and the world watching, Apollo 11 took off from Kennedy Space Center.

After traveling 240,000 miles in 76 hours, Apollo 11 entered into a lunar orbit on July 19. The next day, at 1:46 p.m., the lunar module Eagle, manned by Armstrong and Aldrin, separated from the command module, leaving another astronaut, Collins in the module. Two hours later, the Eagle began its descent to the lunar surface, and at 4:17 p.m. the craft touched down on the southwestern edge of the Sea of Tranquility. Armstrong immediately radioed to Mission Control in Houston, a now-famous message: "The Eagle has landed."

At 10:39 p.m., five hours ahead of their original schedule, Armstrong opened the hatch of the lunar module. As he made his way down the module's ladder, a television camera attached to the craft recorded his progress and beamed the signal back to Earth, where hundreds of millions watched in great anticipation. At 10:56 p.m., as Armstrong stepped off the ladder and planted his foot on the moon's powdery surface, he spoke his famous quote, which he later contended was slightly garbled by his microphone and meant to be "that's one small step for A man, one giant leap for mankind."

Buzz Aldrin joined him on the moon's surface 19 minutes later, and together they took photographs of the terrain, planted a U.S. flag, ran a few simple scientific tests and spoke with President Richard Nixon via communications with Houston. By 1:11 a.m. on July 21, both of the astronauts were back in the lunar module and the hatch was closed. The two men slept that night on the surface of the moon, and at 1:54 p.m. the Eagle began its ascent back to the command module. Among the items left on the surface of the moon was a plaque that read: "Here men from the planet Earth first set foot on the moon—July 1969 A.D—We came in peace for all mankind."

At 5:35 p.m., Armstrong and Aldrin successfully docked and rejoined Collins, and at 12:56 a.m. on July 22, Apollo 11 began its journey home, safely splashing down in the Pacific Ocean at 12:50 p.m. on July 24.

After Apollo 11, there would be five more successful lunar landing missions, and one unplanned lunar swing-by, Apollo 13, (whose lunar landing was aborted due to technical difficulties).

The last men to walk on the moon, astronauts Eugene Cernan and Harrison Schmitt of the Apollo 17 mission, left the lunar surface on December 14, 1972. The Apollo program was a costly and labor intensive endeavor, involving an estimated 400,000 engineers, technicians and scientists, and costing $24 billion (close to $100 billion in today's dollars). The expense was justified by Kennedy's 1961 mandate to beat the Soviets to the moon, and after the feat was accomplished ongoing missions lost their viability. The Apollo missions ended.

Long after he was dead, JFK's speeches were the outline for the future. Space, its exploration and exploitation, was the future. It was our Manifest Destiny to explore space.

I'd never even contemplated the possibility that man never walked on the moon. Even though some evidence didn't seem to add up, it didn't really seem to matter to me. Both fact and fiction pointed to an inevitable future. Why wouldn't a story about such success be true?

But somehow it hasn't quite worked out

as expected. 2017 came and went without not only anymore US trips to the moon and no lunar bases, but also without any other country able to match our accomplishment from some forty-eight years earlier.

It becomes easy to fall into cynicism, to write the whole thing off as a stunt. A one-time geopolitical ploy rooted in a long lost particular-time of history with policy made for reasons which no longer exist. But I want to try not to be cynical. I want to believe.

If I allow myself to fall into cynicism, this leaves us with the ass end of a dream which lives on merely to siphon off public money into some sort of military-industrial government program. Something which exists merely to exist.

When it comes to space exploration, hardnosed taxpayers want to know what they are going to get for their money. Spending billions to plant a flag on some distant point in the universe merely for prestige does not constitute a sound business case which shows a return on investment. You must colonize. That's the foundation of capitalism. Constant expansion is the rule.

So, I started to think that maybe space travel could just be a pipe dream. Something like believing in fairies or unicorns. Something for children which many adults dismiss.

Since the end of the 30 year US space shuttle program in 2011, manned space flight has dwindled to a series of mundane but bone-shaking bus rides on Russian rockets up to the International Space Station in low Earth orbit.

True, NASA is still by far the world's largest space agency, and says it is developing a new generation of manned spacecraft. But a working prototype, let alone a new Apollo style program is many years away.

   Logically, when taking a hiatus, it should provide an opportunity to rethink the whole purpose of sending people into space, which is an environment so profoundly hostile that huge sums must be spent making travel beyond the Earth's atmosphere even remotely safe.

   But too many Americans still feel a compulsion to spend billions of tax dollars on manned space flight, while homeless populations soar and the endless wars continue. When, in 2010, President Barack Obama scrapped the Constellation program that would have taken the US back to the moon by 2020, the storm of protest was intense. It may have been even more intense if everyone realized that we never walked on the moon to begin with.

   In the long and storied history of the United States, a key moment occurred on

August 18, 1805. That day, the "Corps of Discovery", led by Meriwether Lewis and William Clark, crossed the North American continental divide on their way west. Just over a month earlier, on July 4 of that year the crew had drank the last of their whiskey and fired off their guns and hoped that by the time the year was out, they would see the Pacific Ocean. But while the men celebrated the 29th birthday of their nation, the two captains looked anxiously west, and saw huge mountains on the horizon that white people had never-before seen, and wondered how long it would take them to get over them.

Lewis and Clark were very much like the Space Program of today. In fact, the astronauts of the US space program in the 1960's saw themselves as the successors to Lewis and Clark. Primarily military men, assigned on a government mission by a visionary President (in their case, Kennedy), executing their duties with professionalism, for the sake of the nation, not their own personal glory. Lewis and Clark's expedition, the Corps of Discovery, had similar imperatives.

Lewis and Clark, and the country overall held the belief that it was the destiny of the United States to expand its territory over the whole of North America and to extend and enhance its political, social, and economic influence. It was their God given right to take it as their own.

I find America fascinating for many reasons and I'm drawn to the space program and its ancestor, Lewis and Clark, because in my mind it represents that country at its best… and perhaps its worst, when it reached out ahead of time and shows us the world that could be. But perhaps the world that could be is not the world that is. Maybe we do not have a divine right to expand and take what isn't ours?

Moon landing conspiracy theories are theories which claim that some or all elements of the Apollo program and the associated Moon
landings were hoaxes staged by NASA with the aid of other government organizations.

The most notable claim is that the six manned landings were faked and
that twelve Apollo astronauts did not actually walk on the Moon. Various groups and individuals have made claims since the mid 1970's, claims that NASA and others knowingly misled the public into believing the landings happened by manufacturing, tampering with, or destroying evidence including photos, telemetry tapes, radio and TV transmissions, Moon rock samples, and even some key witnesses.

Opinion polls taken in various locations have shown that between 6% and 20% of Americans and 28% of Russians surveyed believe that the manned landings were faked. 50% of Great Britain's doubt the moon landings. Almost 80% of Chinese claim we made the whole thing up.

This is what peaked my curiosity, and inside without bias are the results of ten years of research.

"In an age of universal deceit,

telling the Truth is a revolutionary act."

"Whoever controls the past, controls the future."

–George Orwell–

Chapter 1   *Motivations for Faking*

Lying by omission (by simply not admitting something) may seem less heinous than speaking an untruth directly, but the intent to deceive is the same. Both life and the people in it are complex and rarely have only one reason for doing anything.

In general, I believe lies are told to avoid embarrassment, to protect our interests, to get things we want, to inflate our image, to save time and resources, and to make it seem like we have lived up to expectations when we haven't.

1. Ourselves. lying often to avoid suffering painful consequences, shame, embarrassment, or conflict.

2. Our interests. Probably the second most common reason we lie is to get what we want. We lie to get material goods (like money) and non-material goods (like attention from the telling of tall tales).

3. Our image. We all want others to think well of us, yet we all do have our shortcomings. Rather than admit it, however, and suffer a diminution of others' respect, we often cover it up. We therefore lie to inflate our image, and make ourselves bigger and better than we really are.

4. Our resources. We often lie to avoid expending energy or time or money doing something we really don't want to do (or is impossible to do) but don't feel comfortable admitting.

5. Others. Often a lie is told in order to tell someone what they want to hear, as it will make them happier than

telling them they failed to live up to their expectations in some way.

When examining the above five reasons for lying and cross referencing them to fit in with the 1969 moon landing, it is tempting to construct a paragraph like this:

"NASA lied about landing on the moon in 1969 because they were embarrassed to admit failure. They were getting huge amounts of funding, and all eyes in America were on them. They wanted everyone to see them as successful so that the funding wouldn't stop. They knew that landing and returning an astronaut on the moon in 1969 was impossible, but they needed to live up to their expectations."

The quote "Oh! What a tangled web we weave, when first we practice to deceive" refers to how complicated life becomes when people start lying.

The Apollo 11 mission motivated a generation of innovators, technologists, mathematicians, dreamers, scientists and engineers. It also motivated and brought hope to an entire country. The Moon Landing confirmed that, if you could dream it, promote it, campaign for it, and finance it, almost *anything* could be accomplished.

The Apollo program delivered benefits to 6,300 inventions that we use on a daily basis such as microwave ovens, satellites and satellite technology, and computers and computing to air treatment products and countless other spinoffs. They launched industries such as Intel that were impossible before NASA. And where would the popular breakfast drink Tang be without NASA?

The space program created optimism in the public and in future consumers. Not bad for a program that started when 50% of the US didn't want to fund the Apollo missions.

But if mankind completed so many successful lunar missions, why isn't there a hotel on the moon right now, serviced by daily flights? Generally speaking, after someone achieves the seemingly impossible, everyone jumps on the bandwagon and it becomes commonplace. By comparison, the Wright Brothers flew their first airplane in 1903 and the first commercial flight followed a decade later.

Still why fake the moon landings at all? Could they really have accomplished something like that? What would be the motivation? Accomplishing Kennedy's goal gave society great hope for the future. Putting a man on the moon not only inspired the nation, but also the world. The 1960's were a tumultuous time in the US, and the moon landing showed what could be accomplished at a time when much else was going wrong.

The inspiration provided by the goal of sending humans to the moon is credited for laying the groundwork for, and making widely available, a host of technologies that society depends on today. But what about back then? Let's take a look at the technology.

There were remarkable discoveries in technology such as electrical, aeronautical and engineering science, as well as rocketry and the development of core technologies that really pushed technology into the industry it is today. Great civil technologies were also developed, such as the powdered drink Tang mentioned earlier. Apollo was perhaps one of the greatest engineering and scientific feats of all time. It was huge. The engineering required to leave Earth and move to The Sea of Tranquility required the development of new technologies that before hadn't even been thought of.

And still, it has yet to be rivaled.

Software designed to manage a complex series of systems onboard the capsules is an ancestor to the software that today is used in retail credit card swipe devices. And race car drivers and firefighters today use liquid-cooled garments based on the devices created for Apollo astronauts to wear under their spacesuits. And the freeze-dried foods developed for Apollo astronauts to eat in space are used today in military field rations, known as MRE's, and as part of survival gear.

And those technologies are just a drop in the bucket to importance of the development of the integrated circuit, and the emergence of Silicon Valley, which both were very closely linked to the Apollo program. Of course, they are linked to the military-industrial complex, too.

By today's standards, the information technology Nasa used in the Apollo manned lunar program is extremely basic. Nasa computers were no more powerful than a pocket calculator, yet these ingenious computer systems were able to guide astronauts across 356,000 km of space from the Earth to the Moon and return them safely, or so the story goes anyway. A USB memory stick today is more powerful than the computers that put man on the moon.

Of course, today NASA has over 161 computer racks in its facility with an additional 89 racks for climate simulation. Their computer system is known as the Pleiades, and is one of the world's most powerful supercomputers, which represents NASA's state-of-the-art technology for meeting the agency's supercomputing requirements, enabling NASA scientists and engineers to conduct modeling and simulation for NASA missions. All spacecraft also have computers on board.

The Pleiades has a doozy of a processor using quantum computing for unheard-of calculation speeds 3600 times faster than those of conventional computers. Millions of times faster than the information technology used in Apollo.

Radiation hardening is something that didn't exist back in 1969. Hardening is the act of making electronic components and computer systems resistant to damage or malfunction caused by ionizing radiation, particle radiation, and high-energy electromagnetic radiation. These types of radiation are encountered in outer space and high-altitude flight.

All semiconductor electronic components are susceptible to radiation damage. Radiation-hardened components can reduce the susceptibility to radiation damage. Due to the extensive development and testing required to produce a radiation-tolerant design of a microelectronic chip, radiation-hardened chips tend to lag-behind the most recent developments.

Environments with high levels of ionizing radiation create special design challenges. A single charged particle can knock thousands of electrons loose, causing electronic noise and signal spikes. In the case of digital circuits, this can cause results which are inaccurate or unintelligible. This is a particularly serious problem in the design of satellites, spacecraft, military aircraft, nuclear power stations, and nuclear weapons. In order to ensure the proper operation of such systems, manufacturers of integrated circuits and sensors intended for the military or aerospace markets employ various methods of radiation hardening.

Space Radiation affects all spacecraft. Spacecraft electronics have a long history of power resets, rebooting to safe mode, and system failures due to exposure to radiation, unpredictable solar proton activity, and ambient galactic cosmic ray environment.

The moon is 250,000 miles away. The space shuttle has never gone more than 400 miles from the Earth. Except for Apollo astronauts, no humans even claim to have gone beyond low-earth orbit. When the space shuttle astronauts did get to an altitude of 400 miles, the radiation of the Van Allen belts forced them to a lower altitude. The Van Allen radiation belts exist because the Earth's magnetic field traps the solar wind.

In 2016 NASA said that along with the Air Force they are working to develop radiation hardened processors which would enable computers and telecommunications to work without failure in deep space. But they must have had this in the late 60's, or how did their equipment work?

The two donuts of seething radiation that surround Earthhave been found to contain a nearly impenetrable barrier that prevents the fastest, most energetic electrons from reaching Earth.

The Van Allen belts are a collection of charged particles, gathered in place by

Earth's magnetic field. They can wax and wane in response to incoming energy from the sun, sometimes swelling up enough to expose satellites that are even in low-Earth orbit to damaging radiation. Sometimes even a third belt is formed. The discovery of the drain that acts as a barrier within the belts was made using NASA's Van Allen Probes, launched in August 2012 to study the region. A paper on these results appeared in the Nov. 27, 2014, issue of Nature magazine.

"There are no satellites in these belts, as the computers on-board would be rendered unusable immediately. Beyond the Van Allen Belts lies deep space and the moon. Deep space refers to the frontier beyond Earth's protective magnetosphere and atmosphere where only 24 humans in history, all Apollo astronauts, have ever travelled. No other country has had astronauts go into deep space and return."

Since the end of NASA's celebrated program that saw men walk on the Moon for the last time in 1972, human spaceflight has been limited to low-Earth orbit where the International Space Station is operated inside Earth's natural shielding from high levels of cosmic radiation.

A study compared the mortality rates of lunar astronauts (those claimed to have been in deep space and returned) who have passed away to astronauts who never flew and to those who have only made it to orbit.

The number of cardiovascular disease-related deaths among the deep space astronauts were significantly higher.

The rate among astronauts who never flew is 9%. Among low-Earth orbiting astronauts, its 11%. For the men who claimed travelled to the Moon and deep space, a staggering 43%, or 4-5 times higher than their less-travelled colleagues.

The one exception to the study was Apollo 14 astronaut Edgar Mitchell, who had died after the study's data had already been collected.

"Once you're out of the earth's magnetosphere, and you are in an aluminum can, you are in serious trouble. Protons react violently with aluminum and vice versa so it would destroy the cells in your body much more quickly if you are in a structured aluminum can," said President of Bigelow Aerospace, Robert Bigelow to the Observer during an interview. Bigelow is currently researching and building their own spacecraft. "Our aluminum percentage is very small. We only have aluminum bulkheads and hatches."

Yet, the command module of Apollo was a conical pressure vessel with a maximum diameter of 3.9 m at its base and a height of 3.65 m. It was made of an aluminum honeycomb sandwich bonded between sheet aluminum alloy. The base of the command module consisted of a heat shield made of brazed stainless steel honeycomb filled with a phenolic epoxy resin as an ablative material and varied in thickness from 1.8 to 6.9 cm. At the tip of the cone was a hatch and docking assembly designed to mate with the lunar module.

The skin of the pressurized cabin of the Apollo lunar module was a single wall concept that consisted of 1/8" aluminum.

In interplanetary space, it is believed that thin aluminum shielding would give a net increase in radiation exposure, not only subjecting astronauts to increased radiation levels but rendering all microchip equipment useless.

I believe that all Apollo missions stayed in low-earth orbit.

"One of the saddest lessons of history is this:

If we've been bamboozled long enough,

we tend to reject any evidence of the bamboozle.

We're no longer interested in finding out the Truth.

The bamboozle has captured us.

It's simply too painful to acknowledge,

even to ourselves,

that we've been taken.

Once you give a charlatan power over you,

you almost never get it back."

— Carl Sagan

Chapter 2   *Operation Mockingbird*

On October 30, 1938, the CBS radio network transmitted "The War of the Worlds. The broadcast, directed and narrated by Orson Welles, was based on H. G. Wells' famous novel about a Martian invasion of Earth, but the action was moved from Victorian England to contemporary New Jersey. It was at that time and still is today a brilliant and effective drama, but the broadcast is famous today for reasons that go well beyond its artistic quality.

You might think you know this story. In popular memory, thousands and thousands of listeners mistook a radio play for an actual alien invasion, setting off mass hysteria and panic. The truth was more mundane but also more interesting.

There were indeed listeners who, apparently missing the initial announcement that the story was fiction, took the show at face value and believed a real invasion was under way.

After the play aired, the prominent political commentator Walter Lippmann took the opportunity to warn against "crowds that drift with all the winds that blow, and are caught up at last in the great hurricanes."

The Mars invasion panic cemented a growing suspicion that skillful artists using the proper tools could use communications technology to capture the consciousness of the nation, and get people to believe whatever they intended them to.

To capture consciousness, what a chilling thought that is. This has always reminded me of the fairytale the pied piper.

The pied piper was a rat-catcher hired by a town to lure rats away with his magic pipe. When the citizens refused to pay for his services, the pied piper retaliated by using his instrument's magical power on their children, leading them away as he had the rats. It's an old story that gave me the idea that our leaders are using mass media to brainwash us.

There is also fear among our leaders themselves, who are fretting over the influence of any new medium of communication, such as the internet. If Orson Welles was cast as a wizard with the power to cloud men's minds, his listeners were imagined as a mindless mob easily manipulated.

The fear of conspiracies has been a potent force across the political spectrum, from the Colonial era to the present, in the establishment as well as at the extremes. Conspiracy theories played major roles in conflicts from the Indian wars of the 17th century, from the American Revolution to the War on Terror.

The phrase conspiracy theory was first deployed in the 1960's by the Central Intelligence Agency (CIA) to discredit John F. Kennedy assassination theories. It was imperative that the CIA sell their official story about the assassination and that the American public bought it. But did they?

Theories about JFK's assassination aren't associated with paranoid people wearing tin foil hats. Forty years after John F. Kennedy was shot, an ABC News poll showed 70 percent of the country believing a conspiracy was behind the president's death.

In 2006, a nationwide survey indicated that 36 percent of the people polled — a minority but hardly a modest one — believed it "very" or "somewhat" likely that US leaders had either allowed 9/11 to happen or actively plotted the attacks. That's over one third of the population.

A conspiracy theory is an explanation of an event or situation that invokes a conspiracy without warrant, generally one involving an illegal or harmful act carried out by government or other powerful actors. Conspiracy theories often contradict the prevailing understanding of history or simple facts. The term conspiracy theory is a derogatory one, and those that believe them are scorned and dismissed as crazy, paranoid idiots.

Project MK Ultra which is sometimes referred to as the CIA's mind control program, is the code name given to a program of experiments on human subjects, at times illegal, designed and undertaken by the United States Central Intelligence Agency.

The operation began in the early 1950's, and was officially sanctioned in 1953. Then project then was reduced in scope in 1964, further curtailed in 1967, and officially halted in 1973.

The program engaged in many illegal activities, including the use of unwitting US and Canadian citizens as its test subjects, which led to controversy regarding its legitimacy. MK Ultra used numerous methodologies to manipulate people's mental states and alter brain functions, including the surreptitious administration of drugs (especially LSD), other hallucinating compounds and other chemicals, hypnosis, sensory deprivation, isolation, both verbal and sexual abuse and psychological torture.

Back In 1945, the Joint Intelligence Objectives Agency was established and given direct responsibility for Operation Paperclip. The program recruited former Nazi scientists, some of whom had been identified and prosecuted as war criminals during the Nuremberg Trials.

The primary purpose for Operation Paperclip was for the US to gain a military advantage in the burgeoning Cold War, and later in the Space Race, between the US and the Soviet Union. By comparison, the Soviet Union was even more aggressive in recruiting German during Operation Osoaviakhim. The Soviet military units forcibly and at gunpoint recruited over 2,000 German specialists to the Soviet Union during one night.

Several secret US government projects grew out of Operation Paperclip. These projects included Project Chatter, established 1947, which was a United States Navy program beginning in the fall of 1947 focusing on the identification and testing of drugs in interrogations and the recruitment of agents. Here they would do laboratory experiments on both animal and human subjects.

Established in 1950 was Project Bluebird, which was renamed Project Artichoke in

1951. This again was a mind control program that gathered information together with the intelligence divisions of the Army, Navy, Air Force, and the FBI. Obviously mind control was very important to the government.

These programs are proven examples of overt mind control. They claim that the projects were formed and had grown to counter Soviet advances in brainwashing. In reality, the CIA had other objectives. An earlier aim was to study methods through which control of an individual may be attained. The emphasis of experimentation was "narco-hypnosis", the blending of mind altering drugs with carefully hypnotic programming. They wanted to be able to control people like puppets.

A crack CIA team was formed that could travel, at a moment's notice, anywhere in the world. Their task was to test their new interrogation techniques, and ensure that victims would not remember being interrogated and programmed. All types of narcotics, drugs from marijuana to LSD, heroin and sodium pentothal (the so-called truth drug) were regularly used.

After the invention of the television, which soon became commonplace in households everywhere, a new method of mind control in our so-called free and civilized society became available.

This isn't to say that all things on TV are geared towards brainwashing you. They're not. But most of the programming on television today is run and programmed by the World's largest media corporations. These corporations had interests in defense contracts, such as Westinghouse (CBS), and General Electric (NBC).

This makes perfect sense when you see how slanted and warped the news is today. Examining the conflicts of interest is easily observed when you watch the discussions about an issue, although to understand the multiple ways that lies become truth, we need to examine the techniques of brain washing that the networks are employing.

Radio isn't any different than the TV in its ability to brainwash a population into submission, as we learned earlier using *War of the Worlds* as an example.

Experiments conducted by a researcher named Herbert Krugman revealed that when a person watched television, brain activity switched from the left to the right hemisphere of the brain. The left hemisphere is the seat of logical thought. Here, information is broken down into its component parts and critically analyzed.

The right brain, however, treats incoming data uncritically, processing information in wholes, leading to emotional, rather than logical responses. The shift from left to right brain activity also causes the release of endorphins, which are the body's own natural opiates; thus, it is possible to become physically addicted to watching television. Further studies have shown that very few people can kick the television habit.

It's no longer an overstatement to say that the youth of today are raised and taught to some degree by watching network television, and that they are intellectually dead by their early teens.

Propaganda techniques were first codified and applied in a scientific manner by a journalist named Walter Lippman and a psychologist named Edward Bernays. Bernays was the nephew of Sigmund Freud.

During World War I, Lippman and Bernays were hired by then United States President, Woodrow Wilson, to participate in the Creel Commission, the mission of which was to sway popular opinion in favor of entering the war, on the side of Britain.

Edward Bernays said in his 1928 book Propaganda that, "The conscious and intelligent manipulation of the organized habits and opinions of the masses is an important element in democratic society. Those who manipulate this unseen mechanism of society constitute an invisible government which is the true ruling power of our country."

Operation Mockingbird was allegedly a large-scale program of the United States Central Intelligence Agency (CIA) that, beginning in the early 1950s, attempted to manipulate news media for propaganda purposes, and funded student and cultural organizations and magazines as front organizations. Front organizations can act for the parent group without the actions being attributed to the parent group thereby allowing them to hide from public view.

Approximately 50 of the CIA's assets were individual American journalists or employees of U.S. media organizations. More than a dozen United States news organizations and commercial publishing houses formerly provided cover for CIA agents abroad. A few of these organizations were unaware that they provided this cover, but most knew and were compensated for their involvement.

Also, the CIA currently maintains a network of several hundred foreign individuals around the world who provide intelligence and at times attempt to influence opinion by using covert propaganda. These individuals provide the CIA with direct access to a large number of newspapers and periodicals, scores of press services and news agencies, internet sites, radio and television stations, commercial book publishers, and other foreign media outlets.

As a test, turn on your local newscast. You have a few minutes of blue-collar crime, hardly any white- collar crime, a few minutes of sports, misc. chit chat, random political jibber-jabber, and a look at the viewpoints of their "experts".

The mainstream media openly supports the interests of the military industrial complex and the prison industrial complex. The stories focus on minority criminal groups, and exploit the real threat to appear like they are much more dangerous than they are.

Think about the growing per capita number of prisoners in the country. Then remember that growth happened at exactly the same time that our prison boom began. The police on our streets have created criminals. The focus is to keep us in a state of fear, that way the elitists can attack any group they want to without fear of consequence. This is why the media is continuing to craft the timeless art of dehumanization. It is the media's job to provide propaganda.

It's a tragic day when the state can monopolize on the enslaving and imprisonment of a population.

Hollywood will continue to frighten us with films about the mafia, gangsters, and the corrupt blue collar criminal whose stupidity and greed get them caught. In the end, our minds are already pre-conditioned to accept living in a police state economy and society because we read it in the paper, see it praised on the news and talk shows, or see it in a movie.

So, does mind control exist? Absolutely and without a doubt. But what does that have to do with whether, or not we went to the moon in 1969?

Various groups and individuals have made claims since the mid-1970s, that

NASA and others knowingly misled the public into believing the landings happened. They did this by manufacturing, tampering with, and destroying evidence including photos, telemetry tapes, radio and TV transmissions, moon rock samples, and even some key witnesses.

Many Moon-landing conspiracy theories have been put forward claiming either that the landings did not happen and that NASA employees have lied, or that the landings did happen but not in the way that has been told to the public. The non-believers have focused on perceived gaps or inconsistencies in the historical record of the missions. The foremost idea is that the whole manned landing program was a hoax from start to end. Some claim that the technology to send men to the Moon was lacking or that the Van Allen radiation belts, solar flares, solar winds, coronal mass ejections from the sun, radiation risks from cosmic rays, etc. made such a trip impossible.

As an answer to this, NASA claims that the conspiracy theories are impossible because of their size and complexity. The conspiracy would have to involve more than 400,000 people who worked on the Apollo project for nearly ten years, the 12 men who walked on the Moon, the six others who flew with them as pilots in the command modules, and another six astronauts who orbited the Moon.

To me, NASA's rebuttal does not hold water. Surely a program such as Apollo would have been top secret and extremely compartmentalized, meaning that very few people knew the entire scope of the program, and that there were many smaller sub groups working independently of each other.

If the landings were indeed faked, it would be a crime, and every crime has a motive. One motive might be that NASA faked the landings to forgo humiliation and to ensure that it continued to get funding.

NASA raised about $30 billion to go to the Moon, and that kind of money could have been used to "pay off" many people. Many suggest that the landings had to be faked to fulfill Kennedy's 1961 goal, "before this decade is out, of landing a man on the Moon and returning him safely to the Earth.

In the next chapter, I want to take a look at a motive from a different angle.

"Football, beer, and above all gambling filled up the horizon of their minds. To keep them in control was not difficult."

-George Orwell

Chapter 3 *Cold War and Cold Facts*

A new age has dawned on everyone; an age of remarkable technology. In this new age, we have the ability to scan the heavens and put humans in space. We can divide cells at the sub-atomic level and unravel DNA. We have completed extensive research in Stem cells. We know intimately many of the ways the brain functions; how to shape it, recondition it, influence it, reinforce response mechanisms for a desirable outcome.

This knowledge is immediately recognized and utilized in advertising. The study of human response is big business. These responses include things like how wide the eyes open in the reception of colors and design, facial expressions people make when introduced to new concepts in packaging, and even words people use that denote positive or negative reactions. All of this research is then utilized to introduce new products or to stimulate interest in old ones. It is used by medical and psychiatric hospitals to put patients at ease and by hotels and restaurants to give a pleasurable atmosphere to their customers.

This knowledge is also used by the media for publicizing public figures. They choose the camera angles, edit the script, package the figure they wish to promote or invalidate. This knowledge owes much of its groundwork to a team of scientists brought to the United States from Hitler's Nazi Germany, and protected, while they conducted mental experiments on the US population.

Dr. Josef Goebbels, who became Minister of Public Enlightenment in Germany, aimed to encourage people to support Hitler and, after 1933, to make them into good Nazis. Information was strictly controlled; Germans were permitted to hear only about Nazi strengths and successes. Never were failures discussed.

The Nazi Propaganda Ministry, directed by Dr. Joseph Goebbels, took control of all forms of communication in Germany: newspapers, magazines, books, public meetings, and rallies, art, music, movies, and radio. Viewpoints in any way threatening to Nazi beliefs or to the regime were censored or eliminated from all media. This is proof absolute that people's beliefs can be not only controlled, but molded into visions held by someone else.

In a totalitarian, or police state, the government not only tries to control people's minds and lives but also watches them to make sure its hold on power is never threatened. Fear is used to maintain control.

Enter what I like to refer to as the space-industrial complex. NASA, which many mistakenly believe has been on essential furlough since the moon landings; has actually been prolific in recent years, with **unmanned** missions to Jupiter, Pluto, and Mars. These successes are actually greasing the wheels for new NASA budget proposals.

The agency launched an entire series of novels called "NASA-Inspired Works of Fiction," for which they conscripted science fiction authors to produce novels amenable to what they see as a new eclectic age of federally sponsored space travel.

One of these novels, William Forstchen's 2014 science fiction novel, *Pillar to the Sky*, for example, argues that bureaucratic slashes to the NASA budget are one of the biggest threats to humanity.

The release of the movie The Martian coincided with NASA's request of $19 billion dollars to fund a manned mission to Mars. Great timing, wouldn't you say?

For the record, this is a textbook example of a psychological operation or *psyop* for short. This is a planned operation by the government meant to manipulate public opinion. To put it bluntly, it's a form of propaganda.

Obviously, NASA knows that advertising and movies are a way to sway public opinion. But why would they construct a lie about landing on the moon?

NASA's functions are interwoven with the military-industrial complex, and that should come as no surprise. Since its inception, the Pentagon has controlled the agency through an oversight committee, with the open goal of utilizing the space between Earth and the moon for strategic military operations. Space is widely considered to be the next frontier of warfare. The militarization of space in the coming decades will see tactical satellites capable of launching nukes, disarming weapons, and collecting vast amounts of surveillance data. Control space, and you control the World. So, the possibility is there that NASA is simply a means of covertly directing taxpayer money to the industrial military complex.

Perhaps a real motive might be as simple as this. NASA and the United States Government needed success.

Dancing was a popular activity to do on a weekend in the 1960's. This was the era of the juke box. Teenage males would take their girlfriends out for an evening to impress them with their dance moves and sweep them off their feet. Some moves like The Mashed Potato, The Shimmy, The Swim, The Twist, and The Jerk all came into existence in the 1960's. But it wasn't just a period of endless fun. The 1960's was a decade of social and political upheaval.

Americans who were young in the 1960s influenced the course of the decade as no group had before. The motto of the time was "don't trust anyone over 30." another, "tell it like it is," conveyed a real mistrust of what they considered adult deviousness. Youthful Americans were outraged by the intolerance of their universities, racial inequality, social injustice, the Vietnam War, and the economic and political constraints of everyday life and work.

The 1960's was a period when long-held values and norms of behavior seemed to break down, particularly among the young. Many college-age men and women became political activists and were the driving force behind the civil rights and antiwar movements. For lack of better words, it was a revolution. They became the counter-culture.

The moon landing made people believe anything is possible. This inspired people to go after things they thought was impossible to succeed at. Children looked up to the astronauts as role models. They wanted to do something that was as important to history. Parents wanted to look up to idols such as Buzz Altron and Neil Armstrong.

People could believe that if something bad happened to earth, we could go to the moon and have a shelter there. There would be a new hope for mankind. Also, people believed that if we ran out of resources, then we could go to the moon for more.

Most importantly, people had a new faith in government. The landings helped the United States government distract public attention from the unpopular Vietnam War, and it is somewhat suspicious that the manned landings suddenly ended about the same time that the United States ended its involvement in that war. A successful manned mission to the moon offered a wonderful pride-boosting distraction for the near revolt of the US citizens over 50,000 deaths in the Vietnam War.

After the cold war ended, the ritual enactment of terror theatre continued useful to the western establishment. Europe was once more the focus of a new round of psychological warfare, the *mental* attack that is "terror."

In Europe a group of wealthy elites had long ago sought to replace the remnants and vestiges of traditional culture with masonic atheism, secularism and the Babel of the European Union.

Spiritually dead and rotting from a loss of tradition, it is no surprise the now toxic anti-culture of Europe has been co-opted by the Anglo-American system (through NATO and other globalist entities) to function as a means to both break down both Islam and the vestiges of Christianity through multi-cultural clashes, and migrant movement and relocation. This is a warfare strategy. A great way to do this is by mixing cultures and stoking the fire with synthetic terror.

It is no surprise, then, the thoroughly liberalized populations are unable to cope with the juggernaut of staged terror attacks leveled against them, particularly when faced with establishment aided, funded and engineered terror against its own population. It should be first evident the radical Jihadi model of Al Qaeda and ISIS both share the similar patterns of absurdity, contradiction and Hollywood-esque scripting we've seen in past episodes of Terror Theater. Let's look at the recent Brussels attack.

The recent Brussels attack demonstrates similar patterns to almost all other terror attacks. Before the event, we saw *warnings* of the coming wave of terror and threats from ISIS that these attacks would come. Turkey, you'll recall is a NATO country and likely the origin of much ISIS training and thus the funneling of ISIS into Syria for destabilization. Belgium, of course, is also the headquarters of both NATO and the EU, and despite tips (as is always the case), these tips go ignored. I believe they go ignored because terror is precisely the point.

The date of the Brussels attack was 3/22, which is the number of the masonic lodge known as Skull and Bones, with the second bombing occurring at 9:11 AM. Yes, that time again is 9:11.

There are countless cases of film and television scripting being used for propaganda and staged terror psyops in real covert operations, and this could be one of the more spectacular examples. Also of note are the numerological associations that are not coincidental. It should also be understood that according to the NSA itself in its scholarly publications, numerology and the occult have a long history of usage in cryptography and intelligence communications.

Perhaps the most bizarre and extremely questionable story to come out since the

Brussels attacks, were the reports of Mason Wells, a Mormon missionary, who allegedly survived three separate terror attacks since 2013. He survived the terror attacks in *Boston, Paris and Brussels.*

Back in 2013, just after the Boston marathon bombing, the *Washington Post* ran an article including some interesting statistics about terror directly from the National Counterterrorism Center, which stated that:

> *"In the last five years, the odds of an American being killed in a terrorist attack have been about one in 20 million (that's including both domestic attacks and overseas attacks)."*

A Master number, the 11 is the most intuitive of all numbers. It is instinctual, charismatic, dynamic and capable when its sights are set on a concrete goal. The 11 is the number associated with faith and psychics.

Angel Number 911 is a highly karmic and spiritual number that encourages you to pursue your life purpose and soul mission as a lightworker. It tells of leadership and living life as a positive example in order to illuminate the way for others to follow.

I always associate 911 with endings. you have the 9 number which is the symbol of completion, the triple triad 333, the card of endings before the final number 10, the end of a cycle. Then you have 11 which is the vision, illumination, intuition, and it could also be the double helix. In some numerology 911 is seen as; 9=Endings. 11=DNA. 911=ending code of our DNA. 911 is also a very iconic number now that the symbolism goes back to September 11 where we saw the towers fall. This is the same card in tarot as the Tower. Not to mention all the stories of 911 being an inside job which it WAS so the energy behind the numbers of 911 are pretty symbolic even on the grand scale. 911

marks a very significant day of change within the world. It is about destruction and breaking up the old ways to build the new. Translated, it is to break away from your old structures and habits.

The 911th chapter of the bible is Haggai Chapter 2, and it is the wrath of the Lord on Israel because they had turned away from God and did not come back. Jeremiah 9:11 says "I will make Jerusalem a heap of ruins, a haunt of Jackals." In Jeremiah 19:11, the Lord says he will break this city like one would break a potter's vessel.

Revelation 11:9 says that "Those from the peoples and tribes and tongues and nations will look at their dead bodies for three and a half days, and will not permit their dead bodies to be laid in a tomb. It speaks of Armageddon." Hebrews 9:11 speaks of Jesus, the High Priest, and his return to Earth.

The number 11 is the number of destruction and judgment and the death of man. Any event or thing assigned with the number 11 aids in the raising of the anti-Christ.

Armistice Day/Remembrance Day is November 11 at 11:11 (Triple 11).

The Illuminati (13 Ruling Crime Families) is a ritualistic organization that has been around since the Christian crusades. It has a special way of looking at numbers that we should all know about and uses the numbers for ritualistic witchcraft.

The number code is simplistic. A for example has the number 1 above it, and all through the alphabet this continues until you reach Z, which represents the number 26.

CNN for example would be 3, 14, 14. 3+1=4=1=4 =13. The CIA would be 391. 3+9+1 = 13.

The Illuminati has a very special way of looking at numbers and using them. Pythagoras is the father of numbers and his teachings are venerated by all the mystery schools.

This can be tied in to the ill-fated Apollo 13 mission if you realize there are 13 ruling families in the illuminati, mirrored by 13 members in covens and satanic cults (12 regular members and 1 high priest). This is also mirrored in current day legal proceedings where you have 12 jurors and 1 judge.

To tie this numerology into Apollo 11, 11 is the number of destruction and the deceit and death of man. Any event or thing assigned with 11 is to aid the rising of the Djjal, the anti-Christ. In Latin, the Devil's name is LVX which translates as (50 + 5 + 10 = 65 = 6+5 =11).

When you tie 9 to 11, 9 is the number of divine completion and the number of the fall of man. 9/11 would then translate to the fall of man in a deceitful destruction resulting in death.

"It is easier to fool people

than to convince them that they have been fooled."

-Mark Twain-

Chapter 4 *Risk Assessment and Faith*

For a time, Americans were starting to believe that they were making progress in the space race and that although the Soviets had larger rockets, the United States had better guidance systems. This myth was busted after the Soviets were able to crash *Luna 2* onto the Moon. At that time the closest Americans had come to the Moon was about 37,000 miles (within the Van Allen Radiation Belts) with Pioneer 4 (which was unmanned). Khrushchev, on his only visit to the U.S., gave president Eisenhower a replica of the Soviet pennants that *Luna 2* had just placed onto the lunar surface.

On July 21, 1969, people around the world were glued to TV images of the

Apollo 11 astronauts on the Moon. But space specialists were also tracking the Soviet Luna 15 probe, which had launched three days before the Apollo mission. Luna 15 was just one in a long line of Soviet probes that had made it to the Moon—Luna 2 was the first human-made object to crash into the Moon way back in August 1959 (other Luna missions included the first lunar flybys and the first photographs of the far side of the Moon.

While Neil Armstrong and Buzz Aldrin were supposedly concluding humanity's first Moonwalk, the Soviets made a booboo: their Luna 15 probe crashed into the Moon. The crash site was about 530 miles from the Sea of Tranquility.

The timing of the Luna 15 mission was a little freaky for NASA, as it would orbit the Moon at the same time as Apollo 11, and both would be transmitting radio signals to Earth.

Before the mission, NASA enlisted Apollo 8 commander Frank Borman to get some intelligence on Luna 15's flight plan. Supposedly Borman was friendly with the Soviets, and had just returned from a trip to the USSR. He was the first astronaut to ever go to the USSR.

NASA was concerned that Luna 15 might introduce radio interference if its orbit was too close to that of Apollo 11. But Borman's info from the Soviets confirmed that it wouldn't be a problem, and a worldwide sigh of relief followed.

So we are to take it on good faith that although we were in the midst of The Cold War and a race to the moon, the soviet's willfully gave Borman classified information about their space program. I doubt that this is the case.

Several years ago, Russia's Vladimir Markin, a spokesman for the government's Investigative Committee, said in an op-ed for the local newspaper, Izvestia, that the United States ought to show proof of its historic space journey to the moon. Specifically, Markin wants an inquiry into the 1969 moon walk because videos and a lunar rock from the historic journey have gone missing.

Nasa admitted to losing the video in 2009 and said it was an accidental erase, that officials were only trying to clear up recording space for the tapings of a satellite.

"I don't think anyone in the NASA organization did anything wrong," said Dick Nafzger, a video engineer at Nasa: "It slipped through the cracks and nobody's happy about it."

The slip-up left only grainy images of Neil Armstrong's famous "giant leap for mankind" photo. NASA spent four years searching archives for the lost Apollo 11 mission tapes. This leads me to believe that

Neil Armstrong's giant leap was meant to refer to a giant leap of faith. It is hard to believe that a video of perhaps the largest, most historical event ever could be misplaced or erased.

In August of 2009, the Dutch national museum said that one of its prized possessions, a rock supposedly brought back from the moon by U.S. astronauts, was just a piece of petrified wood.

The Rijksmuseum, more noted as a repository for 17th century Dutch paintings, announced it had had its plum-sized "moon" rock tested, only to discover it was a piece of petrified wood, possibly from Arizona.

The museum acquired the rock after the death of former Prime Minister Willem Drees in 1988. Drees received it as a private gift on Oct. 9, 1969, from then US ambassador J. William Middendorf during a visit by the three Apollo 11 astronauts, part of their "Giant Leap" goodwill tour after the first moon landing. The museum had vetted the moon rock with a phone call to NASA.

Nearly 270 rocks scooped up by U.S. astronauts were given to foreign countries by the Nixon administration. But according to experts and research by The Associated Press, the whereabouts of many of the small rocks are unknown.

NASA turned over the rock samples to the State Department to distribute. "We don't have any records about when and to whom the rocks were given," they claim. Hmmm, no records.

No lunar meteorite has yet been found in North America, South America, or Europe. They undoubtedly exist, but the probability of finding a lunar meteorite in a temperate environment is incredibly low. Note, I said the probability was low. Not impossible. And the possibility that moon rocks could be in rock collections throughout the world is extremely high, although they simply have not been identified as such.

That said, any geoscientist (and there have been thousands from all over the world) who has studied lunar samples knows that anyone who thinks the Apollo lunar samples were created on Earth as part of government conspiracy doesn't know much about rocks. The Apollo samples are just too good. They tell a self-consistent story with a complexly interwoven plot that's better than any story any conspirator could have conceived.

Lunar samples show evidence of formation in an extremely dry environment with essentially no free oxygen and little gravity. Some have impact craters on the surface and many display evidence for a suite of unanticipated and complicated effects associated with large and small meteorite impacts.

But just because some of the rocks are real, does not mean that they were gathered in a manned mission. NASA states as proof that they landed man on the moon between 1969 and 1972 during six Apollo missions, that they brought back 382 kilograms, which is 842 pounds of lunar rocks, core samples, pebbles, sand and dust from the lunar surface.

They claim that six space flights returned 2200 separate samples from six different exploration sites on the Moon. It's important to note here that three automated (unmanned) Soviet spacecraft returned important samples totaling 300 grams (approximately 3/4 pound) from three other lunar sites, proving that moon rocks and samples do not prove that man walked on the moon.

The Soviet Union's *Luna 2* was the second of the Luna programs spacecraft launched to the Moon. It was the first spacecraft to reach the surface of the moon, and the first man-made object to land on another celestial body. On September 14, 1959, it successfully impacted east of Mare Imbrium near the craters Aristides, Archimedes, and Autolycus.

    The *Luna 16* was the first robotic probe (unmanned mission) to land on the Moon and return a sample of lunar soil to Earth after five unsuccessful similar attempts.. It represented the first lunar sample return mission by the Soviet Union and was the third lunar sample return mission overall, following the Apollo 11 and Apollo 12missions. This was in September 1970. It's important to note that it took the Soviet Union 14 more missions after Luna 2 to successfully return a sample to Earth. Apollo, on the other hand ran from 1961 to 1972, with the first manned flight in 1968 (just one year before a successful landing).

    The first Chinese mission to successfully land on the moon was in 2013, again unmanned. It has discovered a new type of volcanic rock on its surface. This finding was the first confirmed discovery from the surface of the moon in about 40 years. The

Chang'e-3 lander gathered rock samples from its landing site in the Imbrium basin. The basin can be seen from Earth and is filled with solidified lava. China's lander deployed its passenger, the Yutu rover, shortly after it landed. The rover last communicated with Earth in October 2015, but since that time has been immobile.

Most people knew that going to the moon was risky business. Some outside of Mission Control, listening to the tense communication between the astronauts and Houston, understood what some of the urgency meant. But few, very few, knew the scope of the dangers that the crew faced. These were no longer theoretical; they were being played out in space at that very moment.

"We would either land on the moon, we would crash attempting to land, or we would abort. The final two outcomes were not good." Well, in 1967 three Apollo astronauts were burned alive on the launch pad. The conclusion of a congressional inquiry was that the entire Apollo program was in shambles and it was a miracle no one was killed sooner. So we are led to believe that all of the problems were supposedly fixed by 1969, just two years later. How could they have made such a large improvement in "quality control" in such a short period of time?

A personal belief of mine is that NASA would not risk broadcasting an astronaut getting sick or dying on live television. The counter-argument generally given is that NASA in fact *did* incur a great deal of public humiliation and potential political opposition to the Apollo program by losing an entire crew in the Apollo 1 fire during a ground test, leading to its upper management team being questioned by Senate and House of Representatives space oversight committees. Since they did incur public humiliation, why would they open themselves to it again? Why would they broadcast a live landing?

    This goes without mentioning that The Soviets had a five-to-one superiority to the U.S. in manned hours in space. They were first in achieving the following seven important milestones: The first manmade satellite in earth orbit, the first man in space, the first man to orbit earth, the first woman in space, the first crew of three astronauts onboard a spacecraft, the first spacewalk, and the first rendezvous of two orbiting spacecraft. Remember, a five-to-one superiority in manned hours. This put America at a perceived military disadvantage in missile technology during the very height of the Cold War.

    The president of the United States at the time was none other than "Tricky Dick" Nixon. He was the king of cover-ups, secret tapes and scandal. Think about other potential antics that were not discovered that occurred while he was in office.

An impeachment process against Richard Nixon was initiated on February 6, 1974, after an investigation showed sufficient grounds and he was later charged with high crimes (felonies) and misdemeanors regarding a cover up.

Life is not so much a battle between right and wrong, as it is a battle between Truth and Lies. Truth leads to good. Lies lead to evil. Life is wonderfully simple.

The simple fact is, *half* of all crimes are *"conspiracies"*. Half are done without forethought, in the heat of the emotion of the moment, and half are plotted out in advance, thus making them conspiracies. Those who would like the public to ignore *half* of all the crimes in the world by ridiculing those with an intellect to perceive such forethought frauds are simply those perpetrating the deceptions in the first place!

Take as an example how a tiny spider, the size of a dime or even smaller, can meticulously plan and trap its prey weeks in advance. If a spider can do that, then the human mind, if inclined to evil, can do so much more evil, so much farther in advance.

Additionally, a lie, or conspiracy, is the only crime that can exist without tangible evidence. If someone is murdered, there is a dead body somewhere. If someone steals, you will have the material possession lacking in one place and existing in another.

Yet, when someone lies, where is it? A lie is the only crime that you cannot touch, that you cannot see. A lie is purely ethereal, which is why lies are the favorite misdeeds of habitual criminals. And out of all the crimes committed in the world for which people are put in prison for, how many of them are there for simply lying? Very few, that's how many. For politicians it's fewer yet.

The origin of crime is the lie,
or conspiracy, invented in advance of the iniquity, to cover up the
wrongdoing before it is even committed.

When crimes are committed on a national and international scale, then national and international lies or conspiracies are needed. The bigger the crime, typically the bigger the lie.

That's why criminal multibillion-dollar corporations and governments have consolidated all television networks, magazines, and newspapers. It is to control your *perception* of reality, not to offer you reality.

It's important to understand that television news stations are *shows* not *news*, and are basically entertainment. Because all of the information is completely controlled from the top down, the anchors (readers) simply regurgitate scripted words from unseen superiors. All the major networks, (ABC, NBC, CBS, FOX CNN, etc.) are receiving the exact same scripts from the very same *central* authority above them.

If in fact the moon landings during the shady Nixon administration were part of a television deception, then you should believe that the CIA played a role in that endeavor, which was entirely presented the media outlets, already proven to be under their direct control. Furthermore, unlike any other event in recorded history, there was absolutely no *independent* press coverage of such a monumental occasion. All newspaper and television commentary and photographs presented to the public were entirely controlled by NASA, the Federal Government, Richard Nixon, and the CIA.

In fairy tales there is always a hero... a Prince Charming. In real life, Prince Charming is the bad guy.

"Obsessed by a fairy tale, we spend our lives searching for a magic door and a lost kingdom of peace."

-Eugene O'Neill

Chapter 5   *Lights, Camera, Espionage, and Chaplin*

Some of the most serious government attacks on personal rights in the United States took place in 1919 and 1920. A large number of government officials took strong, and sometimes unlawful, actions against labor leaders, foreigners, and others. These actions took place because of American fears about the threat of communism. Those fears were tied closely to the growth of the organized labor movement during World War One. There were many strikes during the war. More and more often, workers were willing to risk their jobs and join together in groups to try to improve working conditions.

President Woodrow Wilson had long supported organized labor. And he tried to get workers and business owners to negotiate peacefully.

Public feeling was against the labor unions and political leftists. Many people considered anyone with leftist views to be a revolutionary trying to overthrow democracy. Many state and local governments passed laws making it a crime to belong to organizations that supported revolution. Twenty-eight states passed laws making it a crime to wave red flags. People also demanded action from the national government. The Red Scare did not last long. But it was an important event. It showed that many Americans after World War One were tired of social changes. They wanted peace and business growth.

As the Cold War between the Soviet Union and the United States intensified in the late 1940s and early 1950s, hysteria over the perceived threat posed by Communists in the U.S. became known as the Red Scare. Communists were often referred to as *Reds* for their allegiance to the red Soviet flag.

After American and Soviet troops had greeted each other at the Elbe River toward the end of World War two, Goebbels and Hitler took their own lives rather than be captured by the fast-approaching Soviet forces. Four years after that friendly meeting at the Elbe River, the major capitalist powers transformed the victory over fascism into a "Cold War."

Germany was divided into two rival states, the North Atlantic Treaty Organization (NATO) was formed against the communist movements and the Soviet Union in Europe, provoking a nuclear arms race. In the US, right-wingers organized purges and blacklisting of communists and progressive activists. The decade of the 1940s, one of the most tumultuous in world history, saw ups and downs for communists in the US and in the world.

In Hollywood, a new type of activist had emerged; the actor. With his 1947 film

"Monsieur Verdoux," Charlie Chaplin completed a remarkable transformation from the universally beloved Little Tramp to a vilified monster both on-screen and off.

An icy, elegant black comedy, the film builds to a lengthy philosophical indictment of the sins of modern capitalism. Captured and bound for the guillotine, Verdoux is persuaded by a reporter to deliver a death-row valediction, "a story with a moral." In the ensuing monologue, he declares his own crimes trivial within the context of a murderous society: "As a mass killer I'm an amateur by comparison."

Charlie Chaplin is unique among Hollywood legends for being awarded both an honorary Oscar and the International Peace Prize — the latter being an honor of the World Peace Council, a Communist-led organization. The first award was given to him for being a pioneer of motion pictures, but he was no less the pioneer in his politics. His support for Communist dictators while preaching free speech and tolerance was a sign of what was to come for Hollywood.

In his lifetime, he repeatedly denied being a Communist, saying he was too wealthy to ever want to be one. Instead, he labeled himself "a peace-monger" and supporter of individual rights. Whatever sympathies he had for the Soviets, he asserted, were confined to the war years when Russia was helping defend U.S. democracy against Hitler. Charlie Chaplin was a tortured genius who abused women and was haunted by his childhood poverty.

September 1952 marked Charlie Chaplin's first visit to England in 21 years; yet it also marked the beginning of his exile from the United States. The trip to Europe was meant to be a brief one to promote his new film Limelight, with Chaplin remarking upon his departure that "I shall probably be away for six months, but no more." However, while Chaplin was still at sea, the US Attorney-General announced plans to launch an inquiry into whether he would be re-admitted to the US. In the end, it would be 20 years before he would return.

Celebrities have long been the victims of rumor. Cinema legend Charlie Chaplin was no exception. The British-born actor, who is primarily remembered for his "little tramp" character and who mixed with contemporary notables such as Albert Einstein and George Bernard Shaw, became the subject of a rumor accusing him of being a communist. Chaplin denied being a communist, but never denied sympathizing with the political ideology.

Chaplin recollected in his autobiography that although he was not a communist, he never spoke out against them, which made him guilty in the eyes of the anti-communists.

Chaplin was not alone. The Hollywood blacklist was the practice of denying employment to screenwriters, actors, directors, musicians, and other American entertainment professionals during the mid-20th century because they were accused of having Communist ties or sympathies. Artists were barred from work on the basis of their alleged membership in or sympathy with the Communist Party or refusal to assist investigations into the party's activities. Even during the period of its strictest enforcement, the late 1940s through the late 1950s, the blacklist was rarely made explicit or verifiable, but it directly damaged the careers of scores of individuals working in the film industry.

The Cold War was the geopolitical, ideological, and economic struggle between two world superpowers, the USA and the

USSR, that started in 1947 at the end of the Second World War and lasted until the dissolution of the Soviet Union on December 26, 1991.

The 1950s introduced America to one of the darkest and most illiberal ideas in its political and social history – McCarthyism. The government, and even private enterprise, recklessly accused thousands of Americans of being Communists or fellow travelers and sympathizers, and subjected them to interrogation, investigation and sanctions.

McCarthyism became a broad political and cultural phenomenon that ultimately tarnished the benevolent global reputation of the United States.

The Cold War continued even after McCarthyism was largely exposed as paranoia and self-serving propaganda. John F. Kennedy was elected to the presidency 1960, and shortly after, two crises erupted. In August of 1961, the USSR erected the

Berlin Wall, designed to stem the increasing number of East Germans who were fleeing Communist East Berlin to the West. Then in 1962, the Cuban missile crisis exploded, and the world was a breath away from nuclear war.

    The Cold War brought forth a time of great competitiveness between the United States and the Soviet Union. The Cold War was marked by continuous rivalry between the two former World War II allies. Conflict spanned from subtle espionage in the biggest cities of the world to violent combat in the tropical jungles of Vietnam. It ranged from nuclear submarines gliding noiselessly through the depths of the oceans to the most technologically-advanced satellites in geosynchronous orbits in space. In basketball and hockey, in ballet and the arts, from the Berlin Wall to the movies, the political and cultural war waged by Communists and Capitalists was a colossal confrontation on a scale never before seen in human history.

This competitiveness continued at an alarming pace and it is safe to describe this as: hyper-competitiveness, described as *"an indiscriminate need to compete and win (and avoid losing) at any cost as a means to maintain or enhance* self-worth".

Good competitiveness is the drive to accomplish a goal, to bring out the best in individuals. *Bad competitiveness* is winning at any cost: it sneers at the old aphorism "It's not whether you win or lose, but how you play the game." Losing is for wimps and failures.

What most people don't realize is the extraordinary lengths these people are willing to go to ensure a preservation of the status quo.

Charlie Chaplin was not the only person that saw the value of using film and movies to get a point across. There is an extensive history of the relationship between filmmakers, the Office of Strategic Services (OSS) and its successor, the CIA.

This relationship came to gradually reflect the "breakdown of the consensus vision of American history" or, put more bluntly, how Americans came to stop trusting their government.

The first films were films that dramatized real events and were often made with the cooperation and assistance of OSS head, General William Donovan, and other agency veterans. Unsurprisingly, these celebrated the agency's wartime successes and reflected faith in the "official stories" that government agencies put forth.

For the first decade of its existence, the CIA was virtually absent from the public consciousness and thus enjoyed a golden age of covert action that led to an inflated sense of self-confidence and virtually no oversight.

This era was partly due to CIA policy, which regularly refused to lend its seal of approval to television and film productions, threatened to discourage pictures about espionage and frequently asked studio lawyers to ensure that all direct references to the agency be removed from scripts.

Because the film industry's Production Code also required government approval of any script featuring a state agency, Hollywood tended to use fictional institutions when discussing espionage, until later defamation laws and the weakening of McCarthyism changed the cinematic landscape.

But while filmmakers may have not made films *about* the CIA, at least in the 1950s, they still made films *for* the CIA.

The CIA *"developed a think tank to fight communist ideology, which negotiated the rights to George Orwell's Animal Farm, getting a talking pig on the screen 20 years before 'Charlotte's Web."* The agency pressed for *"line changes in 1950s scripts that would make black characters more dignified, and white characters more tolerant"* in order to promote *"an attractive image of America to a world picking sides in the Cold War."*

Between 2006 and 2011, *VICE* reported the CIA's Office of Public Affairs (OPA)had a role in at least 22 of the U.S. entertainment industry's projects. Some of the productions listed by *VICE* included the films *Argo* and *Zero Dark Thirty*, television shows like *Top Chef* and *Covert Affairs*, and documentaries such as the *History channel's Air America* and the *BBC*'s *The Secret War on Terror*. The book, *The Devil's Light,* also had the help of the CIA. Still, the CIA's involvement in Hollywood is indeed shadowy and difficult to trace, especially since its interactions often take place only between two well-placed individuals, either in person or over the phone.

"All art is propaganda ... sometimes unconsciously, but often deliberately," Upton Sinclair once wrote.

Between 1942 and 1945, during World War II, Walt Disney Productions was involved in the production of propaganda films for the US government. The widespread familiarity of Disney's productions benefited the U.S. government in producing pro-American war propaganda in an effort to increase support for the war. Walt Disney himself was a 33 degree mason.

During World War II, Disney made films for every branch of the US military and government. The government looked to Walt Disney more than any other studio chief as a builder of public morale providing instruction and training the sailors and soldiers. This was accomplished through the use of animated graphics by means of expediting the intelligent mobilization of servicemen and civilians for the cause of the war. Over 90% of Disney employees were devoted to the production of training and propaganda films for the government. Throughout the duration of the war, Disney produced over 400,000 feet of educational war films, most at cost, which is equal to 68 hours of continuous film. In 1943 alone, 204,000 feet of film was produced.

As well as producing films for different government divisions from 1942 to 1943, Disney was asked to create animation for a series of pictures produced by Colonel Frank Capra for the U.S. Army. This series included films such as *Prelude to War* and *America goes to War*. Although these films were originally intended for servicemen, they were released to theaters because of their popularity.

The reason for all of this background is because NASA has been accused of faking the landing's films, saying that they were staged by Hollywood with Walt Disney sponsorship, based on a script by Arthur C. Clarke and directed by Stanley Kubrick.

I should mention that I have been studying the moon landings for years. I've scoured hundreds of sources, books, films, and news stories and after it all my belief is unclear that humans have gone to the moon, but I am convinced that the initial missions we saw on TV were not real, especially Apollo 11.

My research has led me to believe that Apollo 11 was part of a program to get funding for weapon building and a way to illegally divert tax payer money into the military industrial complex.

Once you truly look into all evidence gathered over the period of time since the initial moon landing in 1969, anyone would be forced to reach a truly striking conclusion: it is not clear if it actually happened. The topic has been debated for many years and evidence has been presented on both sides. Looking at both sides of the argument objectively, you could easily walk out with a conclusion on either side – and that's kind of exciting to me.

Unlike the events of 9/11, where the evidence and information available certainly discredits the official story, the moon landings have a different feel entirely.

Kubrick has been linked to the moon landings throughout the research I have done. There have been many theories going around that link Kubrick to the landings, with some even claiming that he tried to reveal the truth in his movie *The Shining* by placing clues in the film, such as the scene in which Danny wears this Apollo 11 sweater.

Also, in the original release of *2001: A Space Odyssey,* there were a number of credits thanking NASA and many of the aerospace companies that worked with NASA on the moon landings. These credits have since been removed from all subsequent releases of *2001*.

One last interesting factor with Kubrick was that his movie *Eyes Wide Shut* was released on July 16th, 1999. Stanley Kubrick insisted in his contract that this be the date of the release. That may not seem interesting unless you know that July 16th, 1999 marks exactly 30 years to the day since Apollo 11 was launched.

Astronaut Alexey Leonov, the first man to walk in space, has said that parts of the Apollo 11 space mission were faked, and that Stanley Kubrick was hired to film them in a studio in Hollywood. I say, if parts were faked, then it would have been easy to fake the whole thing.

"In the end, everything is a gag."

-Charlie Chaplin

Chapter 6   *Houston, we have a problem*

Some of the best evidence suggesting a possible fraud is the fact that in 1998, when the space shuttle flew to its highest altitude ever, 365 miles, one third higher than they normally flew, mission control asked the crew to descend to a lower altitude due to lethal space radiation they encountered, by approaching too close to the Van Allen Radiation Belts, which don't even begin until an altitude of one thousand miles and continue for an additional 25,000 miles.

So, on this particular mission, the astronauts were 635 miles away from radiation that was *so intense*, that the crew reported they could see the radiation with their eyes closed as sparks of light hitting the retinas of their closed eyes, and were subsequently told to descend away from it. When this happened, CNN inadvertently and unknowingly, reported the moon landing fraud by stating . . . "The radiation belt surrounding earth is more dangerous than previously believed."

This statement totally contradicts the authenticity of the "moon landings" . . . Here's why . . .

The *only* time in world history when human beings are *said* to have traveled through the 25,000 mile thick radiation field called the Van Allen Radiation Belts (which, unbeknownst to most, surrounds the Earth starting at an altitude of one thousand miles and extends 25,000 miles beyond that) is during the *alleged* Apollo moon missions, as all other manned missions, from every country on earth including the United States (such as Gemini, Mercury, Soyuz, Skylab, the Space Shuttle, and the current International Space Station), all orbited about 750 miles *below* this dangerous radiation field (merely 250 miles above the Earth's surface), *specifically* out of safety concerns for the lethal radiation above them. Even airline crews, 240 miles below this orbital altitude, are subject to health concerns from this hazardous radiation. This danger is amplified for astronauts *twenty times* higher than airline crews.

Perhaps CNN made a mistake? It wouldn't be the first time.

Today, the newspaper industry and the news networks are disintegrating before our eyes. Thousands of professionals have been laid off, and freelancers who came up in the digital age are used to changing things and altering things. Some professionals also feel that as standards are slipping they can fake and lie and cheat. There is much debate regarding fake images and video footage used by major news networks including Fox and CNN. Mistakes, misrepresentations, and downright deceptions in photojournalism are as old as the practice itself. A lie has speed, but the truth has endurance.

Media disinformation in relation to war is categorized as war propaganda, which constitutes as a criminal offense under international law. But always, they can lie their way out of a jam. A good example of this would be our attacking Iraq and Afghanistan because they were responsible for 9/11, or that Saddam had weapons of mass destruction. These were both lies, war propaganda that was served on a silver platter by the media. The reason they were served was to forward the military agenda, so you have a motive.

CNN became famous for its supposedly live broadcasts during the first Gulf War in 1991, when it sent its journalists - supposedly - to the front lines to cover the drama as it unfolded. In one broadcast, for instance, it appeared as if
then CNN correspondent Charles Jaco and

another reporter, Charles Rochelle, were caught in a potential SCUD attack in the middle of a broadcast.

At one point in the video that CNN was broadcasting, viewers could hear air-raid (or, in this case, missile-raid) sirens going off. A graphic at the bottom-left of the screen said, "Saudi Arabia," while on the bottom-right there was a graphic that said CNN Live. As the sirens wailed, Jaco and the other reporter grabbed "air raid gear" Jaco put on a gas mask while Rochelle grabbed a military-style Kevlar helmet (why both wouldn't have gas masks, since then-Iraqi leader Saddam Hussein had threatened to launch chemical weapons at coalition forces, is not clear - yet).

It all looked and sounded real, of course. But it wasn't.

The next scene featured backstage shots

of the Saudi Arabia "set", an entire news crew, complete with fake props.

Turns out Jaco, Rochelle and their crew weren't in Saudi Arabia at all. They were on a sound set near the CNN headquarters in Atlanta, a faked broadcast that the cable news channel eventually had to quietly admit. There are hundreds and hundreds of such faked broadcasts, all produced to serve an agenda. These types of faked broadcasts are also much less expensive and much safer to produce. Kathy Griffin asked Anderson Cooper if he was a member of the Skull and Bones and he admitted he was on January 1, 2014.

Going back to the radiation discussion, why is it then that Space Shuttle astronauts, some *635 miles away* from this intense radiation, *twenty-nine years after the first "moon mission"*, knew more about the radiation than the Apollo astronauts who *claimed* they were in the middle of it *eighteen times* to the moon and back?

Remember, the Space Shuttle crew's recent discovery proves that this large radiation field is *"more dangerous than previously believed"*. What is *"previously believed"* if not based on the *previous* reports from the "experts" of the radiation field, the Apollo crews, who were *allegedly* the *only* ones in all of world history to have ever traveled through this radiation, with no ill health effects of any kind and no reports of the visible sparks of radiation being seen, as were later reported by the Shuttle crew from 635 miles away! Of course, this is simply *not* possible if the "moon missions" were real. *What does this mean?*

To me, it means that the moon mission astronauts, who *claimed* to have been *inside of* this large radiation field *lied* about being there! Of course, if the "Apollo" crews never went *through* the Van

Allen Radiation Belt, as this contradictory report reveals, then they certainly could not have gone to the moon either, which would require going through the belts!

This is precisely why, nearly fifty years later, all that astronauts from *any* nation on earth can do, *including the United States*, is orbit the earth at about 250 miles altitude. Seeing how the Space shuttle has killed fourteen people just orbiting at 250 miles above the Earth, and that with well proven, three decades newer technology than the "Apollo" program, it is quite a conundrum that thirty years earlier, with antiquated untried machinery, NASA claims to have gone 1000 Times farther, six times, without any fatalities whatsoever, and that with antique equipment.

According to the highly esteemed National Research Council, a private nonprofit scientific think-tank which submits recommendations to NASA based on the latest scientific findings, radiation *beyond Earth orbit* is so dangerous that "returning to the moon" is deemed impossible until better ways are found to protect astronauts from this lethal radiation. Yet no astronaut that went to the moon ever got radiation poisoning.

The question is, if the NRC says that "returning" to the moon is impossible *today* until better ways are found to protect astronauts from lethal space radiation beyond earth orbit such as the Van Allen Radiation Belts, then how did men reach the moon on their *very first attempt* with *1960's technology*, or better still, why not simply use the same outstanding methodology that the supposed first moon crews had to protect themselves from lethal space radiation rather than reinventing the wheel?

I recall sitting in science class in Jr. High school, as my teacher passed around a small piece of mysterious material to the class. "This is from NASA," she exclaimed.

"You can pull it all you want and it won't tear, but you can poke a hole in it. Please don't." Of course, a fellow classmate Kurt Smith put his pencil through it immediately. This material was paper thin, silver in color, and was used on the lunar module.

When George Bush Jr. was president, he went on national television and proclaimed that *"The United States will return to the moon as a logical first step to Mars and beyond"*. If they already *really* went to the moon *six* times, why would they need to do a "first" step over again for the seventh time? He was even so bold as to go on to say that *"First we will need to learn how to protect astronauts from lethal space radiation."* Am I the only one curious enough to ask, "Why not do it the same way that worked so well the first time they went to the moon?"

Still, nobody wants to connect the obvious dots, because the dots may lead to a *horrific Truth* that would appall the *entire* American citizenry, demanding that their government be reformed. It is because "journalists" are part of the CIA's media empire that they do not report anything that would cause their very own undoing.

The CEO and founder of Amazon is today the owner of The Washington Post. When the national political "newspaper of record" is owned by a business partner of the CIA, every word on its pages should be suspect. Washington Post owner Jeff Bezos is in financial bed with a cloak and dagger agency that tells lies for living, yet the public is expected to believe his newspaper. Bezos' technicians at Amazon are building information "clouds" for the CIA -- while his reporters discharge clouds of disinformation at the *Post*.

Even for a multi-billionaire like Bezos, a $600 million contract is a big deal. That's more than twice as much as Bezos paid to buy the *Post* four months ago.

And there's likely to be plenty more where that CIA largesse came from. Amazon's offer wasn't the low bid, but it won the CIA contract anyway by offering advanced high-tech "cloud" infrastructure.

Bezos personally and publicly touts Amazon Web Services, and it's evident that Amazon will be seeking more CIA contracts. Last month, Amazon issued a statement saying, "We look forward to a successful relationship with the CIA."

The history of the CIA's involvement with the American press continues to be shrouded by an official policy of denial and deception for the following principal reasons:

The use of journalists has been among the most productive means of intelligence-gathering employed by the CIA. Although the Agency has cut back sharply on the use of reporters since 1973 primarily as a result of pressure from the media, some journalist-operatives are still posted abroad.

Further investigation into the matter, CIA officials say, would inevitably reveal a series of embarrassing relationships in the 1950s and 1960s with some of the most powerful organizations and individuals in American journalism. So don't look!

In the 1950s and early 1960s, Time magazine's foreign correspondents attended CIA *briefing* dinners similar to those the CIA held for CBS. In 1965-66, an accredited Newsweek stringer in the Far East was in fact a CIA contract employee earning an annual salary of $10,000 from the Agency. As common sense would show, a nation of sheep will soon have a government of wolves. The people were being led astray.

People believe what they want to believe, much of the time. I don't mean to say that they believe things without any reason, but they believe, often-times, without good reason.

Most people will give some reason why they believe something. But an indicator of the fairness of their point of view is how they respond to even-handed, fair criticism of their view and to evidence for an opposing view. Lots of people have reasons for what they believe, but when those reasons are refuted--when they're taken away or weakened by other evidence--do they still stand on their point of view, or are they willing to adjust their view based on the evidence that comes in? Usually they are not.

The Misconception is that when your beliefs are challenged with facts, you alter your opinions and incorporate the new information into your thinking. The Truth is that when your deepest convictions are challenged by contradictory evidence, your beliefs get stronger. This is how we are wired. It's a defense mechanism.

Many people believe that the moon landing is basically the adult version of Santa Claus or Father Frost, the Easter Bunny and the Tooth Fairy. But it is not the lie itself that scares people; it is what that lie says about the world around us and how it really functions. If NASA was able to pull off such an outrageous hoax before the entire world, and then keep that lie in place for four decades, what does that say about the control of the information we receive?

"If You Don't Read the Newspaper You Are Uninformed, If You Do Read the Newspaper You Are Misinformed."
-Mark Twain

Chapter 7   *Rocket Man*

The Apollo 11 mission was the first successful manned lunar mission, launched from the Kennedy Space Center, Florida. The power behind this flight was the Marshall Space Flight Center developed Saturn V launch vehicle or rocket, in laymen's terms.

This launch took place on July 16, 1969 and safely returned to Earth on July 24, 1969. The Saturn V vehicle produced a holocaust of flames as it rose from its pad at Launch complex 39. The 363 foot tall, 6,400,000 pound rocket hurled the spacecraft into Earth parking orbit and then placed it on the trajectory to the moon for mans' first lunar landing. Aboard the space craft were astronauts Neil A. Armstrong, commander; Michael Collins, Command Module pilot; and Edwin E. Aldrin Jr., Lunar Module pilot.

Apollo 1 was designated to be first manned mission of the Apollo Program. The mission was scheduled to fly on February 21, 1967, to test the Apollo Command/Service Module (CSM) but it never made it to the launch date because of a cabin fire during a launch rehearsal at Cape Canaveral Air Force Station Launch Complex 34, on January 27, 1967. This accident claimed the lives of NASA astronauts Gus Grissom, Ed White and Roger Chaffee.

On April 4, 1968, just one year and three months before this mission was Apollo 6. This was the final unmanned test for the Saturn V rocket before it would carry a three-man crew around the moon and back, and things did not go as planned. Two minutes and five seconds into launch, the rocket was severely shaken by "pogo oscillations", variations in thrust caused by changing fuel rates. Pogo oscillations were named after the bouncy pogo stick children's toy. In a series of unrelated flaws, parts flew off the lunar module adapter and two of the five engines shut down prematurely during the second stage burn. Apollo 6 did manage to reach space, but never made it to its planned 100-mile circular orbit. Later, the third rocket stage would also fail to reignite.

The Saturn V was the brainchild of Dr. Wernher von Braun. A German, von Braun worked for the Nazis during World War II creating the V2 rockets fired on London. He later surrendered and came to the United States following the war, designing the Saturn V for NASA. On Thursday, September 20, 1945, Wernher von Braun arrived at Fort Strong. The small military site on the northern tip of Boston Harbor's Long Island was the processing point for Project Paperclip, the government program under which hundreds of German scientists were brought into America. Von Braun filled out his paperwork that day as the inventor of the Nazi V-2 rocket, a member of the Nazi party, and a member of the SS who could be linked to the deaths of thousands of concentration camp prisoners. Two and a half decades later, on Wednesday, July 16, 1969, von Braun stood in the firing room at Kennedy Spaceflight Centre and watched another of his rockets, the Saturn V, take the Apollo 11 crew to the Moon. The Saturn V stands 363 feet tall, about 60 feet higher than the Statue of Liberty.

After working in relative obscurity in New Mexico for four years, von Braun and other former Nazi scientists brought overseas under Project Paperclip were moved to the US Army's Redstone Arsenal in Huntsville, Alabama. On March 22, 1952, von Braun introduced the American public to his vision of space exploration in the pages of *Collier's Magazine*. In a series of articles published over two years, he described how men would live and work in huge doughnut-shaped orbital space stations before setting off on missions to the Moon. Years before the Soviet Union launched Sputnik, von Braun worked closely with Disney Studios and even directed the animators and designed Disneyland's Tomorrowland ride called Rocket to the Moon. Also, von Braun hosted the Disney show *Man in Space*. His co-host was Heinz Haber, another NASA Nazi. Haber worked for Strughold and co-authored papers that were based on human experiments performed at Dachau and other concentration camps in which hundreds of prisoners were subjected to experiments that simulated the conditions of high speed, high altitude flight. Prisoners that survived the experiments were generally killed, then dissected. When the Eisenhower administration asked Disney to produce a propaganda film regarding the peaceful uses of nuclear energy, Haber was picked to host the Disney show, "Our Friend the Atom." Haber then wrote a popular children's book of the same title.

Nazi expertise and propaganda in faking film footage has been so entwined with NASA that is conceivable that such expertise was employed during the Apollo missions. Another Nazi scientist who became an American space hero was Dr. Hubertus Strughold, later called "the father of US space medicine." He had a long and distinguished career at NASA an even had an American library named after him. He ran a facility at Dachau in which medical experiments were carried out on prisoners and he even had a traveling laboratory, going from camp to camp. He came over in Operation Paperclip.

One area of Strughold's research was a precursor to the CIA's MK Ultra mind control experiments, in which drugs were used on prisoners. But the Nazi-NASA connection that relates to my Apollo program concerns is the Nazi penchant for fabrication and deceit, and the Hollywood connection.

Fritz Lang was the legendary German filmmaker who created *Metropolis* and the more obscure *Frau im Mond*, which translates to "woman on the Moon."

Hermann Oberth, considered the "Father of the Space Age," was the technical consultant on rocketry in the film. They filmed a dummy rocket being dropped down a chimney, and then ran the footage in reverse, creating the illusion of a rocket taking off. They created a promotional film that combined footage from real tests with Lang's film and passed off the whole thing as a documentary.

When they finally got a rocket to fly as it should, von Braun took that footage, combined cartoon footage with it, and produced a movie extravaganza that gulled a skeptical Hitler in 1943. Hitler was so impressed with what he saw that he bestowed a professorship on von Braun and devoted all possible effort into developing the V-2. They failed to tell Hitler that nearly all of their rocket launches were still failing.

The Gestapo confiscated Lang's models for his film. The situation is similar to what conspiracy theorists think may have been the dynamics surrounding the Apollo missions. I believe that the FBI and CIA investigated the Apollo 1 fire and that the FBI destroyed all blueprints of the Apollo spacecraft and Saturn rockets.

To make interstellar travel believable NASA was created. The Apollo Space Program presented the idea that man could travel to, and walk upon, the moon. The working theory is that every Apollo mission was carefully rehearsed and then filmed in large sound stages at the Atomic Energy Commission's Top Secret test site in the Nevada Desert and in a secured and guarded sound stage at the Walt Disney

Studios within which was a huge scale mock-up model of the moon.

In the late 1960s, von Braun's genius supposedly gave us the Saturn 5 and put us ahead in the space race. The Soviets failed in their efforts to build intricate booster rockets of the type that supposedly put the first US astronauts into a lunar orbit in 1968. It is said that Von Braun's Saturn rockets eventually took 27 Americans to the moon, 12 who walked on the lunar surface. Von Braun retired from NASA in 1972 and died five years later. But who was Apollo?

Apollo was a powerful God which had inspired several "demonic" or Abyssic Gods. Known as Helios by Nero Caesar, Phoebus or "Shining," Apollo is the twin brother of Artemis (Diana). His center of worship was at Delphi which was renowned throughout the ancient world for its oracular advice delivered by a priestess called the Pythia the Chthonic serpent/dragon. Nero Caesar actually considered himself a manifestation of Apollo as he was the God of Illumination, Light, Music, Medicine and more. His arrows sent plague and death which earned him the Biblical name of Apollyon or Abaddon, the King of the Bottomless Pit, better known as Lucifer. "Apollo" is another name for Satan or Lucifer, and this is an interesting choice NASA made as a title for its Moon missions.

There are people claiming to possess special enlightenment or knowledge of something. These people are known as the illuminati. On May 1, 1776, was the most important date in Freemasonry's Luciferic New World Order plans. On that date an obscure Jesuit-trained professor of canon law at the University of Ingolstadt in Bavaria, Adam Weishaupt, founded a secret society called the *Ancient and Illuminated Seers of Bavaria* (AISB for short).

This Illuminati was founded on a mixture of Masonic secrets (Luciferic Doctrine), Islamic Mysticism (Sufism), and Jesuit mental discipline (Hatha Yoga). A unique and dangerous element was the illuminati's scientific use of the drug, hashish, to produce an "illuminated" state of mind-derived directly through the Knights Templar's association with the Order of the Assassins.

Illumination had long been a cherished component of Masonry and other occult groups. The Masonic candidate requests, and is promised "light in Masonry." As he goes up the ladder of initiation, he receives "more light". It is because of this society's emphasis on illumination that the AISB became known by its more common title, the Illuminati. This illuminati is composed of those whose intellectual and spiritual perceptions have revealed to them that civilization has secret destiny, and the outcome of this secret destiny is a *World Order* ruled by a King with supernatural powers.

All names, missions, landing sites, and events in the Apollo Space Program echoed the occult metaphors, rituals, and symbolism of the Illuminati's secret religion. The most transparent was the faked explosion on the spacecraft Apollo 13, named "Aquarius" (new age) at 1:13 (1313 military time) on April 13, 1970, which was the metaphor for the initiation ceremony involving the death (explosion), placement in the coffin (period of uncertainty of their survival), communion with the spiritual world and the imparting of esoteric knowledge to the candidate (orbit and observation of the moon without physical contact), rebirth of the initiate (solution of problem and repairs), and the raising up (of the Phoenix, the new age of Aquarius) by the grip of the lions paw (re-entry and recovery of Apollo 13). 13 is the number of death and rebirth, death and reincarnation, sacrifice, the

Phoenix, the Christ (perfected soul imprisoned in matter), and the transition from the old to the new. Another revelation to those who understand the symbolic language of the Illuminati is the hidden meaning of the names of the Space Shuttles, "A Colombian Enterprise to Endeavor for the Discovery of Atlantis... and all Challengers shall be destroyed." The working theory is that exploration of the moon stopped because it was impossible to continue the hoax without being ultimately discovered. And, of course they ran out of pre-filmed episodes.

In December of 2014, NASA sent their brand new *"Orion"* spacecraft, *un-manned*, directly into the Van Allen Radiation Belt, at a 3,600 mile altitude, and then promptly u-turned it for a return to earth. If you are curious about what is worth studying at *3,600* miles, think about deep space and the Van Allen Radiation Belts.

According to NASA, the purpose of the "Orion" mission was to . . . "to test some instruments". What "instruments" were onboard the Orion spacecraft? Geiger counters; and they were used to measure the radiation inside of the radiation belts. Didn't NASA already have these measurements decades ago from the Apollo moon missions, if indeed men had actually gone through the radiation belts eighteen times to the moon and back? Why was it so important to "test the instruments" at a 3,600 mile altitude inside of the radiation belts? To see if humans can survive trans versing it .

Apparently, today's *new* generation of NASA engineers, some in their twenty's, have stumbled upon this significant NASA contradiction. Though they were probably led into the space exploration field by the motivation of the *seemingly* easy "moon missions" of the 1960's, the fact that such an acclaimed feat cannot be repeated today, with technology that has continually advanced for five decades, and that aside from theses *alleged* "moon missions" of the Nixon administration, no one has ever gone more than 400 miles away from the earth in the nearly fifty years since, the trip to the moon being 1000 Times farther, must look at this just a little closer.

Kelly Smith, a youthful engineer, was selected as the official *"Orion"* mission spokesperson in a NASA video press release. At 43 seconds into the filmed press release, Smith confirmed that the radiation belts are made up of *"Extreme Radiation"*. At time 3:06 he *again* referred to the belts as *"Dangerous Radiation"*. Finally, at time 3:36, for the *third* time, Smith plainly stated, *"We must solve these (radiation) challenges before we send people through this region of space."*

The question is, if the solution to the dangerous radiation belt problem has *yet to be invented* (*"We must solve these *challenges before we send people through this region of space."*), then how is it that the Apollo crews during their alleged moon missions went through this dangerous and extreme radiation nearly *fifty years ago,* when the necessary equipment to survive doing so has not been invented yet?

"If you tell a big enough lie and tell it frequently enough, it will be believed."

Adolf Hitler

Chapter 8 *It's Witchcraft*

During 10 days in Earth orbit, Apollo 9 conducted the first manned flight test of the Lunar Module, demonstrating its propulsion and ability to rendezvous and dock with the Command Service Module. An extravehicular activity (or EVA) tested the Portable Life Support System.

On July 20, 1969, the Apollo 11 Lunar Module performed the first manned landing on the Moon in the Sea of Tranquility, overcoming navigation errors and computer alarms. Astronauts Armstrong and Aldrin performed a single EVA in the direct vicinity of the Lunar Module. Both 9 and 11 involved the lunar module.

    Again, Apollo was one of the most important and complex of the Olympian deities in classical Greek and Roman religion and Greek and Roman mythology. Apollo became associated with dominion over colonists, and as the patron defender of herds and flocks. Yes... I said dominion over colonists. According to some scholars the words are derived from the Doric word *apella* (ἀπέλλα), which originally meant "wall," or even more precise "fence for animals." The role of Apollo as god of plague is evident, with the purpose of sending a plague against the Greeks. A lot of temples dedicated to Apollo were built in Greece and in the Greek colonies, and they show the spread of the cult of Apollo.

    Isopsephy is the Greek word for the practice of adding up the number values of letters in a word to form a single number.

Isopsephy is related to qematria, the same practice using the Hebrew alphabet, and the ancient number systems of many other peoples. A gematria of Latin-script languages was also popular in Europe from the Middle Ages to the Renaissance, and its legacy remains in numerology and Masonic symbolism today.

From the numerological point of view, it is understandable why *Apollo 11 landed on the moon first*. 11 is a very strong number, and it has an indispensable impact on the world. Number 11 is a master number. A master number consists of 2 digits and it doubles the meaning of the corresponding single-digit number. The meaning of number 11 is assigned to leadership skills, intuition, and inspired missionaries.

There is a belief that Apollo's 11 launching date - *July 16, 1969* – is connected with Illuminati influence. It is not surprising because landing on the Moon is the event worth of their intermediation.

Making some numerological calculations:
July 16, 1969 1+6 =7; July = 7; 1+9+6+9 = 25

The only one NASA capsule that didn't reach the assignment was Apollo 13. This mission collapsed because of the explosion in the oxygen tank that blocked the work of the mechanism. The date of the mission was on April 17, 1970.

Number 13 is considered to be unlucky in numerology, and we can see it on the Apollo's 13 example. The time of propel was at 14:13 on April 11, 1970 and the sum of digits in this date makes 39 which is triple 13. In Texas, where the launching was made, the actual time of start was 13:13.

The numbers "9" and "11" have had significant meaning throughout our history.

The birth of Jesus Christ is the one of the most significant events in all of history and when we understand the truths regarding the true date of his birth it will thrill and inspire your heart. Tradition has made December 25th the birthday of Jesus. but the Bible clearly reveals he was not born on that day. It was not until the 4th century after Christ that December 25th began to be celebrated as the day of Christ's birth. It was the old pagan holiday celebrating the winter solstice and the birth of the sun god and celebrated when the days began to get longer. In Rome, it was the festival called Saturnalia and later the Roman Empire baptized it and began to celebrate it as the birth of Jesus. All biblical scholars know that Jesus was not born on December 25th. Tradition is never an accurate measurement for truth. Most scholars now agree Christ was born on September 11th.

9 Knights Templar banded together in 1111AD and maintained the original 9 for 9 years. Centuries later, on 9/11/19 the U.S invaded Honduras and on 9/11/22 was the British mandate in Palestine. On 9/11/41 was the ground-breaking ceremony for the Pentagon, which would 60 years later be

one of the "terrorist" targets. Then on 9/11/73, Salvador Allende of Chile, the world's first democratically elected Marxist president, was overthrown by the US in an admitted CIA coup engineered by Nixon, Helms, and Kissinger; the same Henry Kissinger that was originally to head the 9/11 commission "investigation" (cover-up).

The USA-backed overthrow or coup of Chile in 1973 spearheaded by Kissinger and Nixon was also on Sept 11. The event started with a bang as rebels bombed the Palacio de La Moneda, the presidential palace, with British-made jets. So, we have USA-backed bombings of an important government building in Chile by jet planes (or symbolic doves, as we shall see) on another Sept 11

11 years before the 2001 attacks, on 9/11/90, President Bush gave his State of the Union Address about the New World Order, mentioning it several times. The next year on Sept. 11th he gave another speech

regarding a New World Order. Exactly 7 years before 9/11 on Sept. 11th, 1994, just after 11pm, a single-engine Cessna was stolen then flown into the side of the White House. Needless-to-say, this date September 11th seems to have some historical synchronistic significance with U.S./Britain and their imperial agenda. However, the numerology surrounding this event is not restricted to just its date/history.

September 11th (9+1+1 = 11) is the 254th day of the year (2+5+4 = 11) which means there are 111 days left in the year.

New York was the 11th state to endorse the constitution and New York City has 11 letters. World Trade Center buildings 1 and 2 were 110 stories tall. That's 11 +0.

The Freemasonic Statue of Liberty that was placed near the Trade Center stands on an 11-pointed star pedestal. The number "11" itself is two pillars side by side like the twin towers. It was even an American Airlines (AA = 11) Flight 11 carrying 11 crew members that allegedly hit the north tower.

What were the flight numbers on September 11, 2001? Flight 175 = 1 + 7 + 5 = 13, Flight 11, flight 77, Flight 93 left gate 17. And you all actually thought that radical Muslims with plastic knives and box cutters did this? Then you must be brainwashed.

One of the planes had 93 (13x3 = 39 reversed 93) passengers and crew, another had 58 passengers (5+8=13). United Airways (UA – 21, 1 = 2+11 = 13) Flight 175 (1+7+5 = 13) had 56 passengers (5+6 = 11).

On Sept. 11th, Bush Jr. announced an 11-day national state of mourning. Then 11 days later, on Sept. 22nd he presented the Patriot Act before Congress. The Patriot Act is the unconstitutional 10,000-page anti-terror legislation supposedly written with super-human speed between Sept. 11th and Sept. 22nd.

On 9/11, Flight AA11 (11:11 encode two tower symbology) is hijacked and flown into the 93rd floor of North tower. Then just after, Bush Jr. reportedly tells the school principal, "a commercial plane has hit the World Trade Center and we're going to go ahead and do the reading thing anyway."

And so Bush starts reading "My Pet Goat" At 9:03am UA (13) Flight 175 (13) hits the South tower at the 77th floor and that news is whispered in Bush's ear. A half hour later Flight 77 crashes into the Pentagon, and an hour later Flight 93 crashes in Shanksville, in Pennsylvania.

"Pan in mythology is the Angel of the Abyss, his song shall end the world, and he started playing it on September 11th, 2001, when he was set free during the 9/11 super-ritual. In Faust we learn that the Pentagram is not Satanic at all, but rather a protective symbol placed over the Abyss by the angels of Heaven. But when one of the sides of the

Pentagram wore off due to the passage of time, the symbol turned into a portal, and the Devil was set free to wreak havoc unto this world. You know, like when Flight 77 crashed into the side of the Pentagon."

Exactly 6 months after 9/11 on 3/11/02 the New York sky was illuminated by 88 (8x11) flood-lights to remember the victims. The lights shone straight upwards (like the digit 11) forming two blue pillars of light publicly said to be a tribute to the people lost in the towers. This was done for exactly 33 days, from 6:30 to 11:00pm.

Then exactly 911 days after 9/11, on 3/11/04 were the Madrid "terrorist" train bombings! Reportedly there were 191 (1+1+9 =11) deaths which also encodes 911.

On this same day, 3/11/04, World Trade Center owner Larry Silverstein bought the 110-story Sears Tower valued at $911 million dollars. Then, exactly 911 hours after the Madrid train bombings, the April 19th, 2004 Chicago Sears tower "terrorist" attack was thwarted!

The next "terrorist" bombing was the July 7th, 2005 (7/7/2+5 = 777) London Subway bombing which occurred precisely 444 days after the Sears tower attempt.

The blasts went off at 8:49am which is 11 minutes to 9. On 11/9/05, the Amman, Jordan "terrorist" hotel bombs killed 38 (3+8 = 11). On 7/11/06 in Mumbai India another "terrorist" train bomb killed 209 (2+9 = 11) commuters, using 7 bombs spaced exactly 11 minutes apart from first to last blast (77).

To this day we celebrate this Armstice as Veterans Day every year on the 11th. Just after 9/11 the movie Oceans 11 was released 12/7/01 (1+2+7+1 = 11). The "Two

Towers" Lord of the Rings movie featuring an evil all-seeing eye enemy came out the following year 12/19/02 (1+2+1+9-2 = 11 and 12+19+2 = 33). The trilogy starts with Bilbo's 111th birthday party.

Let's examine representations of various eleven's woven into this terrible tragedy.

1. The first 11 is formed by the day on which this tragedy occurred, September 11.

2. The second 11 is formed by adding the 9th month, September, and the date, (9 + 1 + 1), forming another 11.

3. The third 11 is formed by the airplane number that first crashed into the World Trade Tower. That plane was American Airlines Flight #11.

4. The fourth 11 is formed by the airplane number that crashed into the Pentagon.

That plane was United Airlines Flight #77 (11 x 7).

5. The fifth 11 is formed by the North Twin Tower of the World Trade Center was 110 stories tall (11 x 10).

6. The sixth 11 is formed by South Twin Tower, the World Trade Center was 110 stories tall (11 x 10).

   The seventh 11 is the two towers themselves standing side by side. Satanists love to express their beliefs and their goals in architecture. Thus, many of the buildings of Washington, D.C., were created originally with occult symbols on them, and in them. This fact is the reason why the street designs are created in such a way as to form Satanic symbols. The streets north of the White House form an inverted Pentagram, the Goats-head of Mendes, while the streets joining the White House to the Capitol form one side of a Masonic

Compass, while other streets form the Masonic Square and Rule.

   Another '11' is formed by one of the doomed flights, where the crew totaled '11'.

   The ninth '11' is formed by the fact that September 11 is the 254th day of the year. When you add 2 + 5 + 4 you get '11'

   The tenth '11' is formed because, after September 11, there are 111 days left in the year.

   The eleventh '11' is formed by the historic fact that New York State was the 11th state to join the Union in preparation to create the 13-state confederation that would declare independence from England.

   Mohammed's birth is celebrated on the 11th day of the 9th month. (9/11). 119 is the area code to Iraq/Iran. 1 + 1 + 9 = 11. The Twin Towers - standing side by side,

looks like the number 11. The number of stories is 110 (2x) 110 – 110. Remember that the zero "0" is not a number, so we have 11:11. The number of Tower windows = 21,800. 2+1+8+0+0 = 11. The third building #7 to fall had 47 stories = 4+7=11. The first plane to hit the towers was Flight 11. American Airlines phone number was 1-800-245-0999.
1+8+0+0+2+4+5+0+9+9+9=47 = 11

New York City has 11 Letters. Afghanistan has 11 Letters. The Pentagon has 11 Letters. Ramzi Yousef (convicted of orchestrating the bombing attack on the WTC in 1993) has 11 Letters.

George W. Bush has 11 Letters. Flight 11 - 92 on board - 9 + 2 = 11. Flight 11 had 11 crew members. Flight 77 had 65 on board . 6 + 5 = 11. The Flight 11 call letters were AA11: A=1, A=1, AA=11.

Four of the hijackers on flight AA11 have the initials A. A. for their names: AA=11. The fifth AA11 hijacker was the pilot, Mohamed Atta, 11 letters, and AA in last name.

Flight AA11 had 92 people on board - 9 + 2 = 11. Flight AA11 had 11 crew members - 2 pilots and 9 flight attendants.

Manhattan Island was discovered on Sept. 11, 1609 by Henry Hudson -11 letters. Trade Center is 11 letters, and Skyscrapers is 11 letters. World Trade Center Towers is 22 letters - 2 x 11 =22. The WTC Twin Towers - standing side by side, look like the number 11.

The first WTC tower hit (North Tower) collapses at 10:28 A.M. -1+2+8=11. The 1st Fire Unit to arrive to the WTC towers was FDNY Unit 1. Unit 1 lost 11 firemen. The WTC towers collapsed to a height of 11 stories.

After 99 days of burning, NYC declares the WTC fires are extinguished - 9 x 11 = 99. The World Trade Center fires burn continuously for 99 days, between September 11, 2001 and December 19, 2001. The World Trade Center fire is the longest burning commercial fire in U.S. history.

On September 7, 2002, NYC Medical Examiners announced the revised official death toll from the World Trade Center attacks was 2,801 - (2+8+0+1 = 11).

On the morning of September 11, 2002, the names of 2,801 victims were read at a Ground Zero Ceremony. It took 2 ½ hours to read all the names.

According to the FBI, earlier terrorists originally planned to hijack 11 planes. Thirty days after the attack, the FBI released a Most Wanted Terrorist List with 22 names.

Mohammed, the prophet of the Muslim faith, died in 632 A.D. - 6+3+2=11. The Taliban's Manual of Afghan Jihad (Holy War) is 11 volumes. The League of Arab States is comprised of 22 Arab nations - 2 x 11 = 22.

The suspected base of the terrorists is Afghanistan - 11 Letters. Osama bin Laden's birthplace was Saudi Arabia - 11 letters, whom I might add are now legally responsible for 9/11.

The Prime Minister of Israel - Ariel Sharon - 11 Letters. Deputy PM, & Minister of Foreign Affairs for Israel - Shimon Peres - 11 Letters.

On Friday 9-13-2001, President George W. Bush went to the WTC to talk with and thank the Firefighters, rescuers, and police officers who have given their time and hearts tirelessly 24 hours a day since the horrible tragedy. President Bush stood on top of a pile of rubble with a firefighter whose helmet was numbered 164. 1+6+4 = 11.

The train which was stopped and two suspected terrorists arrested near San Antonio, Texas was #121 = 11 x 11. American Airlines or AA - A=1st letter in alphabet so we have again 11:11. The house where the terrorists are believed to have lived was # 10001. (don't count the zeros).

In the Holy Bible, both Babylon is fallen and the great city is fallen. If you implant the words (World Trade Centers), she has become a home for demons. She is a hideout for every foul spirit, a hideout for every foul vulture and every foul and dreadful animal. When they see the smoke of her burning, dust on their heads, saying: "Alas, the *Great City*...For in (only) one hour she has been laid waste! The (capitalist) merchants...who gained wealth from her...stand back in fear...weeping and mourning." -Revelations 18 (9)

Nostradamus said: "In the City of God there will be a great thunder, Two brothers (towers?) will be torn apart by Chaos, while the fortress endures, the great leader will succumb", The third big war will begin when the big city is burning. At forty-five degrees, the sky will burn, Fire to approach the great new city: In an instant a great scattered flame will leap up."

Michel de Nostredame, better known as Nostradamus, was a French physician and reputed seer who published collections of prophecies that have since become widely famous. Below are interpretations of 4 quatrains of Nostradamus, which I feel accurately predict the Apollo Moon landings will be hoaxed.

I'll start with the well-known quatrain which has commonly been interpreted as predicting the Moon landing

9 - 65

"He will come to go into the corner of Luna,"

Where he will be captured and put in a strange land:

"The unripe fruits will be the subject of great scandal,"

"Great blame, to one great praise."

This quatrain is usually interpreted as a prediction of a genuine Moon landing. But I believe it predicts a hoaxed Moon landing much more accurately.

The first two lines describe an astronaut who intends to go to the Moon, or is under that assumption. Instead, he is taken (captured) and put onto a fake Moon stage set (a strange land). It's clear that Nostradamus is making a distinction between a genuine landing and a hoaxed landing. Otherwise, "He will go into the corner of Luna" would suffice to describe a genuine landing. But it's clear that he will come to go to the Moon, and then he will be captured and put somewhere else.

The third line - the "unripe fruit" refers to the Apollo rockets, which are not advanced enough to fly astronauts to the

Moon. It may have a second meaning as well. Gus Grissom - NASA's top astronaut - hung a large lemon on the side of the Apollo I capsule. This was his 'message' to the gathered media that the capsule was a "lemon", just like one may call a car that's a piece of junk, a "lemon". Grissom died in that capsule, soon afterwards, in a massive fire.

The last line - "Great blame" for the hoax (and perhaps for Grissom's death) would go to NASA, of course. The "great praise" goes to "one". That suggests the praise goes to one person. That person is - Gus Grissom. I'll explain this further with the other moon hoax quatrains .

To my knowledge, the following three quatrains have never been interpreted as predictions of a Moon landing hoax. These are interpretations that I found through research.

An interesting point about these quatrains - they are placed together, in sequence, in Centuries. Its known that Nostradamus, as a general rule deliberately shuffled his quatrains, so they would have no chronological order, or readily identifiable pattern. If two or more quatrains described the same event, they were placed in separate sections of Centuries. They were not grouped together.

So, to have three quatrains in sequence, all describing the same event, is a rare exception to that rule. Perhaps the only example of it. I think Nostradamus had a purpose in keeping them together, as I'll explain after my interpretations.

4 - 29

"The Sun hidden eclipsed by Mercury

Will be placed only second in the sky:

"Of Vulcan Hermes will be made into food,"

"The Sun will be seen pure, glowing red and golden."

The "Sun" is Apollo, the Greek Sun god. In fact, all of the Apollo astronauts wore a patch of the Sun god Apollo on their spacesuits.

Apollo (the Sun) is hidden, eclipsed by Mercury. Of course, he cannot mean the actual planet Mercury, since it does not hide or eclipse the Sun.

Nostradamus is referring to the Mercury space capsule. It went into a sub-orbital flight. Apollo went into low-Earth orbit, which is slightly higher than sub-orbit. Hence, the Apollo capsule is "hidden" from view, "eclipsed" by the Mercury capsule.

The second line now makes sense:

Mercury was placed first in the sky (in sub-orbit). The Sun (Apollo) "will be placed only second in the sky" (in low-Earth orbit).

Third line:

Hermes was the messenger of the Greek gods (such as Apollo). He delivered their messages to the mortals. Hermes was also the traveler of boundaries, and the guardian/protector of all travellers. Vulcan was the Roman Sun god. "Of Vulcan Hermes will be made into food," means Hermes is burned to death.

So who is Nostradamus describing as Hermes?

Gus Grissom. The astronaut who hung a lemon on the Apollo I capsule, as noted in Quatrain 9-65. The messenger of the god Apollo. He sent messages to the mortals (the public) that NASA was hiding the truth about Apollo. He refused to keep silent, so he was burned to death (made the food of Vulcan) in the Apollo I capsule.

Fourth line:

Hermes (Grissom) now dead, the truth is kept from the public. Thus, the Sun (Apollo) will be seen pure, glowing red and golden.

To sum up:

Line 1, Apollo (the Sun) is hidden. That changes by Line 4, when Apollo becomes "seen" as pure, golden.

Grissom's death (Hermes) by fire made the public's deception possible

4 - 30

"More than eleven times the Moon will not want the Sun,"

Both raised and lowered in degree:

And put so low that one will stitch little gold:

"After famine, plague, the secret will be discovered."

The first line is simply brilliant. Exceptional.

The "Sun" is Apollo, as before. More than 11 times, the Moon ("will not want") Apollo. That is, more than eleven Apollo missions will not reach the Moon.

Apollo 11 was by far the most famous, (supposedly) putting the first man on the Moon. So, Nostradamus chose the number eleven, to emphasize the specific mission recognized as the 'pinnacle of human achievement' - Apollo 11 - was also hoaxed, and did not reach the Moon.

Second line: Apollo never goes higher than Earth orbit, at varying altitudes ("degrees").

Third line: "and put so low that one will stitch little gold" Apollo is "put so low" - only intolower earth orbit that it will "stitch little gold" - that it will not the great achievement they claim it to be.

Fourth line: Nostradamus predicts that the hoax will eventually be revealed to the world.

4 - 31

"The Moon in the full of night over the high mountain,"

The new sage with a lone brain sees it:

"By his disciples invited to become immortal,"

"Eyes to the south. Hands to his breast, his body in the fire."

This quatrain is about Gus Grissom.

First and second lines:

Grissom "sees" the Moon. He realizes the truth is being hidden about the Apollo Moon missions.

Third line:

Grissom was chosen by NASA and his peers ("his disciples") to become famous, for all history regarded as the first man on the Moon - "to become immortal".

Fourth line:

Nostradamus describes perfectly how Grissom (and crew) were positioned in the Apollo I capsule, when they died in the fire. Grissom's charred body was still seated when they later opened up the capsule. His hands were still grasping at the safety harness strapped to his chest.

Now, remember earlier that I mentioned Apollo was associated with dominion over colonists. There is an esoteric, but hidden and encoded meaning of the name "Eagle" for the lander. The cabalistic ritual script called for elevated man, initiated god-man, to "ride" the black phoenix bird, the "Eagle," to glory, upward toward the sun. God-man was to make his nest among the stars which decorate the black-garbed night, amidst the day-time canopy of the blue sky (the blue lodge).

Virtually everything that NASA does is permeated with magic and alchemy. Moreover, the real purpose of NASA is contained in another matrix, hidden from the public at large. This process involves the creation of Satanic ritual magic enabling the Illuminati elite to acquire and accumulate power even as the mind-controlled and manipulated masses are pushed into ever increasing states of altered consciousness.

It begins to look more and more like the widely publicized successful flights and missions-and even the staggering tragedies such as the fate of the crews of the ill-fated Challenger and Columbia space shuttles-are masterfully scripted theatrical productions. It is all Grand Theater, hoodwink, in which some rather harmless rites are made public to deceive and charm the profane masses; while others, more sublime and evil, are concealed and known only to the elite, while keeping "the animals" fenced in.

"The scariest monsters are the ones that lurk within our souls."
-Edgar Allen Poe

Chapter 9 *Something on My Mind*

In the bible, the apostle Paul says that Satan masquerades as an angel of light:

> *And no marvel; for Satan himself is transformed into an angel of light (2 Corinthians 11:14).*

One example of this masquerading is the culture of secret societies that claim to have illumination or light but are in fact full of darkness. Their Gnostic teaching inverts the truth, making Satan the god and God the enemy.

> *The true name of Satan, the Kabalists say, is Yahweh (GOD) reversed; for Satan is not a black god, but a negation of God...the Kabala imagined Him to be a "most occult light.*

Once you understand what is going on in the world you can then recognize evidences of *Satanism* in so many, many places. It was proven from Masonic books that Masons worship both Lucifer and Satan. They serve both the "good" Lucifer and the "evil" Satan. They believe that both good and evil exist in equal measure in the world. They also believe good cannot exist without an equally powerful evil.

This belief is the reason we see both type of 5-pointed stars within Masonry; the star with the upright single point is a symbol of the "good" Lucifer, while the star with the two points upward is a symbol of the "evil" Satan. It also takes 33 degrees of rotation of a pentagram to achieve a Satanic pentagram.

A Mason (or Freemason) is a member of a fraternity known as Masonry (or Freemasonry). A fraternity is a group of men (just as a sorority is a group of women) who join together because: There are things they want to do in the world.

Of the claims that Freemasonry exerts control over politics, perhaps the best-known example is the New World Order theory, but there are others. These mainly involve aspects and agencies of the United States Government.

It is a known fact that Freemasons intertwine various symbols and numerology into modern culture, such as corporate logos. Also, the United States was founded by Freemasons who have interwoven Masonic symbols into American society, particularly in national seals, streets in Washington, D.C., architecture, and the dollar bill.

Several founding fathers such as George Washington, Benjamin Franklin and James Monroe were Freemasons. This alone is astonishing, because in 1820 only roughly five percent of males in the united states were masons. In fact, roughly one third of the United States Presidents have been Freemasons.

Barack Obama made a stunning announcement on the 42nd Anniversary of Gus Grissom's death:

CAPE CANAVERAL — President Barack Obama will ask Congress to extend International Space Station operations through at least 2020 but abandon NASA's current plans to return U.S. astronauts to the moon, administration and NASA officials said Wednesday.

This scuttled the Constellation program. The obvious reason for the announcement could be the economy (which certainly isn't hurting the ballooning defense budget), but the *timing* of the announcement still raises my antennae. Could the scuttling of Constellation mean that the dream of manned space flight is a thing of the past? A secret admission of the inhibiting power of the Van Allen Belt?

If we needed a smoking gun of Obama's (alleged) obsession with a martyred Masonic spaceman, we couldn't do much better than that. Grissom was Obama's childhood hero, but also was a relentless critic of NASA rocket engineering, which he considered to be unsafe and unsound.

Grissom, piloting Liberty Bell 7 become the second American to go into space on July 21, 1961. That flight popularly known as Liberty Bell 7 was a sub-orbital flight that lasted 15 minutes and 37 seconds that nearly killed the veteran test pilot when explosive bolts prematurely detonated sinking the capsule.

On January 27, 1967 while training for what would be the first Apollo mission (AS-204) a fire was sparked in the oxygen rich capsule which killed Grissom and his two fellow Astronauts Edward White and Roger. That mission was renamed Apollo I in honor of the crew.

Grissom was a member of Mitchell Lodge number 228 of Mitchell, Indiana.

Freemasons have been involved since the beginnings of NASA. If there was a group who could pull of a great hoax to fool nearly the entire planet, it would be possible through the Freemasons.

An inordinate number of NASA astronauts, the current propagators of the globalist heliocentric doctrine, are or were admitted Freemasons as well. John Glenn, two-time US senator and one of NASA's first astronauts is a known Mason.

Buzz Aldrin Jr. is an admitted, ring-wearing, hand-sign flashing 33rd degree Mason from Montclair Lodge No. 144 in New Jersey.

Edgar Mitchell, another supposed moon-walker aboard Apollo 14 is an Order of Demolay Mason at Artesta Lodge No. 29 in

New Mexico. James Irwin of Apollo 15, the last man to lie about walking on the moon, was a Tejon Lodge No. 104 member in Colorado Springs.

Donn Eisele on Apollo 7 was a member of the Luther B. Turner Lodge No. 732 in Ohio. Gordon Cooper aboard Mercury 9 and Gemini 5 was a Master Mason in Carbondale Lodge No. 82 in Colorado.

Virgil Grissom on Apollo 1 and 15, Mercury 5 and Gemini 3 was a Master Mason from Mitchell Lodge No. 228 in Indiana.

Walter Schirra Jr. on Apollo 7, Sigma 7, Gemini 6 and Mercury 8 was a 33rd degree Mason at Canaveral Lodge No. 339 in Florida. Thomas Stafford on Apollo 10 and 18, Gemini 7 and 9 is a Mason at Western Star Lodge No. 138 in Oklahoma.

Paul Weitz on Skylab 2 and Challenger is from Lawrence Lodge No. 708 in Pennsylvania.

NASA astronauts Neil Armstrong, Allen Sheppard, William Pogue, Vance Brand, and Anthony England all had fathers who were Freemasons too!

The number of astronauts known to be Freemasons or from Freemasonic families is astonishing. It is likely that more astronauts and people of key importance in NASA are affiliated with the brotherhood as well, but not so open about their membership. For there to be this many Masons, members of the world's largest and oldest secret society, involved with the promotion and propagation of this globalist heliocentric doctrine from its outset to today should raise some serious suspicion!

C. Fred Kleinknecht, head of NASA at the time of the Apollo Space Program, is now the Sovereign Grand Commander of the Council of the 33rd Degree of the Ancient and Accepted Scottish Rite of Freemasonry of the Southern Jurisdiction. It was his reward for pulling it off!

All of the first astronauts were Freemasons. There is a photograph in the House of the Temple in Washington D.C. of Neil Armstrong supposedly on the moon's surface in his spacesuit holding his Masonic Apron in front of his groin.

On the outside, the Freemasons claim to be a fraternity, nothing more than a big boy's club, while many claim that it is behind the doors of societies such as that of the Freemasons, that politics and many important world issues are dictated and decided. It is most notably coined a "society with secrets" rather than a secret society.

They are only one of many secret societies in the world today; however many that we are familiar with today have their roots in masonry, even those claiming to anti-masonic. I am not about to claim that the Freemasons are the source of the world conspiracy, but we have taken a look at what ties them to it.

I believe that the masons are controlled by those international bankers who are the more powerful controlling forces directing the bringing about the New World Order. It is well understood by most Christian organizations and thus, right wing organizations, that Masonry is indeed part of that effort to create a New World Order, and that masonry has down through the ages played an important part.

The purpose of "no boundaries, no religion, and One World Government", is to enslave the 95% of the masses, for 5% of the rulers of the world, and that slavery is not really so bad compared to war that has happened in free countries during the past century.

If you oppose the New World Order, then the alternative would be continued war. But the wars themselves have been financed and controlled by these same 5% of the people who have ruled in the past, and the 5% will now be rulers in the future and the 95% will be totally disarmed and without any power such as voting, or any chance of throwing off the yokes of poverty. This awareness indicates the trick has always been, if you want to change people to get them to take certain bait, then you create fear over here, create a problem to make them run from it, so that they will go to that which is the trap you have set for them. Therefore, you herd them into the pen or trap, and they think they have escaped something terrible.

Abraham Lincoln declared martial law during the Civil War. Martial law has not been lifted yet from his declaration of martial law, over a hundred and fifty years ago. This results in a system where, anytime entities in power want to do something that is illegal under the Constitution, they simply go ahead with it under the principle of the martial law declared by Lincoln. That is how the Executive Orders are presented. They are Executive Orders based on martial law that has not been lifted. This is also referred to as admiralty law.

As a result, you have, in one period, a war on poverty. A few years later you have a war on drugs. And there are more and more of these wars occurring every two years. Otherwise, Martial Law would have to be canceled and you would be back under the Constitution, and your freedoms could be restored.

You could then plead Constitutional Rights in courts of law. However, at present, the courts of law are following Admiralty Law, and therefore, if you plead Constitutional Rights in court, you are not likely to get anywhere.

Astronaut Gordon Cooper, one of the original seven Mercury astronauts, confirmed the existence of a mind control program administered by NASA in the 1950's and 1960's involving gifted American schoolchildren. These children were known as "The Space Kids."

The space kids were children with exceptional mental abilities run through a kind of MK program that emphasized cultivation of the children's psychic abilities involving telepathy, remote viewing, and out-of-body-experiences (OBE's).

These students are now in their thirties, forties, and fifties, and are recovering memories of unusual classes that they were enrolled in as young children during the advent of the Space Age.

These "study groups" included speed reading lessons that enabled students to comprehend entire passages at a single glance, the use of learning machines to teach them vast amounts of information, card games and other situational exercises involving clairvoyance, and seminars in the guided imagination that forms the basis of remote viewing.

The man tasked with the development of NASA's Space Kids Project was an infamous super spook doctor and ESP (Extrasensory perception) guru, Dr. Andrija Puharich. Dr. Puharich was a mind control merchant who sold his services to the highest military intelligence bidder.

NASA had been supporting Dr. Puharich's research in ESP since the 1950's. He had a close personal relationship with NASA's director, SS Werner von Braun, and astronaut Master Mason Edgar D. Mitchell, a research associate. Dr. Puharich was a man shrouded in mystery, controversy, and the secret cult of military intelligence too heavy to cover in any detail here.

In 1978, Puharich's assistant, Valerie Ransone, was working with Walt Disney to expand the Space-Star Kids Project. Smoke and mirrors, Ransone claimed to be in touch with extraterrestrials and UFO's.Ransone said: "We're putting together a network…to help design a new landscape for tomorrow."

So Ransone was working at Disney, and if you remember In the 1950s, Wernher von Braun worked with Disney Studio as a technical director, making three films about space exploration for television. Walt Disney visited von Braun at Redstone Arsenal in Huntsville, Ala., in 1954.

Perhaps this is how the world was sold and LOST in "space" back in the 1950's. The whole world became Disneyland.

Walt Disney himself went out of his way to show off all the wonderful world of technology he created to make us believe cartoons were really moving. Now, keep in mind Disney was a Mason.

Back then it was space as product to sell to the masses. An opiate. A fiction to believe in like Santa Claus. Pushed by what "WE" can accomplish. But there is no "WE" in the corporate entity we know as the "USA". It's all set up. There is no real capitalism, its feudalism really. It's all rigged behind the scenes. Disney is, I believe a very important part of the puzzle.

What is the greatest cover-up in history? Can one discovery change the destiny of humanity and restore sanity and harmony to the planet? Who is behind the thrones of governments, religion, science and big business? Is the "New World Order" really something new? Is there an occult history of America and the world? Why do governments and religions and businesses use occult symbolism?

Over 30,000 surviving ancient texts refer to alien visitation. Can they all be wrong? Have we been told the truth about our origins, our forefathers and Earth's past? Have you been told the truth about NASA?

When a recent bizarre event was captured on film showing what appeared to be dark skyscrapers floating in the clouds above China, the world was puzzled. While scientists were quick to dismiss the occurrence as a mirage, not all agreed.

In the days after the event, one particular conspiracy theory started to gather serious momentum — the belief the sighting was the result of a secret NASA mission known as Project Blue Beam.

Canadian journalist and conspiracy theorist Serge Monast first developed the theory in 1994, before publishing his beliefs in a book entitled Project Blue Beam.

The theory suggests NASA and the United Nations are planning to create a new world order by using technologically simulated mind control to shape a global New Age religion.

Mr Monast believed generating a global New Age religion was the only thing that would make a worldwide dictatorship possible.

STEP 1: The breakdown of all archaeological knowledge
Mr Monast detailed his belief that NASA would aim to discredit all existing religions through the breakdown of all archaeological knowledge.

STEP 2: A gigantic space with 3D holographic laser projections

Mr Monast said the second stage in creating a new world order would be using a gigantic space show with 3D holographic images, lasers and sounds to seduce people into believing in the new god.

STEP 3: Telepathic two-way communication
This is where things start to get really creepy.
It is believed NASA will use low frequency radio waves to telepathically communicate with humans in an attempt to shape their beliefs to match those taught by the New Age religion.

STEP 4: Universal supernatural manifestations using electronic means
The final step of Project Blue Beam is to create chaotic event that will leave people willing or desperate enough to accept the new world order.

As you would expect with such a highly contentious topic, there are strong beliefs supporting and discrediting the conspiracy theory. Each of the four stages has evidence suggesting they are under way, although it is possible these things are just a coincidence. Keep in mind it was the CIA that created the label "conspiracy theorist" to attack anyone who challenges the "Official" narrative. As Thomas Jefferson once said; *"A country cannot be both ignorant and free..."*

"There is nothing more deceptive than an obvious fact."
-Arthur Conan Doyle

Chapter 10 *A Moonwork Orange is Shining*

In 1968, one year before the Apollo 11 mission, 2001: A Space Odyssey which is an epic science-fiction film was released. This film was produced and directed by Stanley Kubrick. The film involves themes of existentialism, human evolution, technology, artificial intelligence and extraterrestrial life. The film is best known for its scientifically accurate depiction of space flight, pioneering special effects, and ambiguous imagery.

2001: A Space Odyssey initially received mixed reactions from critics and audiences, but it garnered a cult following and slowly became the highest-grossing North American film of 1968. It was nominated for four Academy Awards and received one for special effects. The special effects were stunning, leading people to regard the film maker Stanley Kubrick as a 'genius' and one of the greatest visionaries of the 20th Century.

In the public's collective minds, *2001* was supposed to resonate about the transcendence to a higher realm...but that was forever changed into 9/11! We will not remember the future and ascension to higher consciousness. Instead, *2001* will mean a *stab* to our psyche; several terrorist attacks, and war; and hate; and revenge; and a giant leap backwards. *2001* will stand for all the wrong things it was never supposed to symbolize.

Immediately, the thought strikes you that *2001* with all those lunar sets was filmed in 1968 and directly after was the Moon landing in 1969. So, I began to think of the county's leaders at the time, the same leaders that made people think that a lone gunman was responsible for killing President Kennedy.

It's not that much of a stretch to think that the Illuminati, or New World Order were confident *they* could pull ANYTHING off. In my mind, this is the exact same mind-set that executed the demolition of the NY Twin Towers in 2001, while we were told it was a terrorist attack. The point is...those that control the media and everything else...can get away with anything and most everybody will believe the lies. But, in time...the truth, eventually, becomes known.

Perhaps the government had something on Stanley Kubrick. Was he obliged to help the feds because they allowed him access to the Pentagon during the filming of Dr. Strangelove? Could they have had private films of Kubrick in compromising positions?

Whatever the reasons, Stanley Kubrick may have taken a bite from of Satan's Apple. Maybe they made promises of backing any future film that Kubrick wanted to make

There are actually three theories about the United States landing on the moon. The first theory is that we went, and that the moon landing photos and film are genuine. The second theory is we went, but all the photos and filming was staged and done here on Earth. The third theory is we never went at all. Over time, after giving each theory a chance, one realizes more and more evidence-to-proof that the lunar missions (we saw) were 100% phony and a *Grand Deception was pulled over the eyes of the world.*

The public is largely unaware that *Kubrick admitted to filming the Moon landings*; and that for his efforts he was given the *Keys to the Kingdom* for his efforts. Could it be that he was trying to tell us the truth in later films?

A documentary titled "Shooting Stanley Kubrick" was created by filmmaker T. Patrick Murray, which claims that Kubrick, who was notorious for avoiding interviews, granted him one on March 4, 1999, purportedly to discuss his soon-to-be-released film "Eyes Wide Shut" and the rest of his large body of work. Instead, fueled by Johnny Walker Blue, Kubrick confessed the following:

"I perpetrated a huge fraud on the American public, which I am now about to detail, involving the United States government and NASA, that the moon landings were faked, that the moon landings ALL were faked , and that I was the person who filmed it."

Before Murray could run out and tell the world, Kubrick allegedly made him sign an

88-page nondisclosure agreement stating that the admission would be kept secret until 15 years after his death. Kubrick passed away three days later, making 2014 the year it could finally be released.

    My belief is that NASA was so desperate to beat Russia in the space race, that they contacted director Stanley Kubrick to shoot a fake landing, so they could at least *appear* to have beaten them to the surface of the Moon. The evidence for this, where it fits in with Kubrick, is that there are apparent signs of the lighting technique known as 'front projection' in the infamous NASA Moon landing video, which Kubrick had pioneered for use in movies like *2001: A Space Odyssey*. I have a degree in film from Penn State University, and have actually run a photographic studio for an advertising agency in New York City. I'm not saying that this makes me an expert, but I do know quite a bit about film. The evidence is there. I also know enough about film to say that Stanley Kubrick was an incredible genius and artist that the world has not fully appreciated.

In another of his films, *The Shining*, released 11 years after Neil Armstrong walked on the 'Moon, you see a film that is heavy with symbolism that suggests Kubrick was confessing his secret. Symbolism like Little Danny Torrance wearing the film's biggest clue: a jumper with the Apollo 11 rocket knitted right into the pattern. It's hardly subtle and suggests that Kubrick really wasn't doing such a great job at keeping quiet.

One change from Stephen King's book that Kubrick saw fit to make was to change the number of the iconic room in the Overlook from Room 217 to Room 237. The reasons for this are obvious, apparently: the average distance between the Earth and the Moon is 237,000 miles. Room 237 represents the fake lunar landing set, The Overlook Hotel represents America and

Danny, who approaches the room, represents Stanley Kubrick's artistic side.

The page that Jack leaves behind at the typewriter? Cast iron *proof* that Kubrick faked the Moon landing. Where you see the word "All", as in *All work and no play makes Jack a dull boy*, "A11", simply is short for Apollo 11. Apparently, this line is an insight into Kubrick's mental condition: that working on the Apollo 11 'project' and having to keep it a secret had made him go a little crazy.

If Jack Torrance represents Kubrick, then Shelley Duvall's Wendy represents Kubrick's own wife, Christina. The scene in which Wendy confronts Jack about his behavior and suggests he has to quit has parallels with Kubrick's own secret. Jack's response? "That is so typical of you!... I've made an agreement... I have obligations to my employers!" It's so blatant.

In the film, there are also the iconic hexagonal pattern found on the carpets in the Overlook Hotel, which look like they were designed specifically to reference the Apollo 11 launching pads. This is how Kubrick effectively owns up to his engineering of the biggest fakery in human history: via carpet samples? Skeptics say no way, but I definitely see a pattern here.

Danny sees the corpses of twins in one scene which could be a reference to *Gemini*, the NASA missions before Apollo (remember the Gemini twins). There were seven Apollo space missions, but only six landed; in the hotel's kitchen, where there are six crates of the soft drink 7-Up. Dick Halloran comes from Florida, which is where Apollo 11 was launched. The owner of the hotel has an eagle on his windowsill; the Apollo 11 lunar module was nicknamed 'The Eagle'. The truth is out there! If you look hard enough!

This extraordinary analysis of *The Shining* is what is most stunning to me. My original fears from this horror movie are now replaced by a far more sinister force, because *it* operates in the real world with the NWO. Symbols of what was really happening at NASA are revealed in the man's astounding, visual art. If you've ever noticed the differences between King's book and Kubrick's movie, we can now comprehend why there were odd differences from the book to the film.

Going back to *2001*, it is very interesting that from the beginning to the end of the film, that it perfectly parallels the development of the Apollo Space Program. And in watching the effects, you have to keep in mind that they were done in a time before blue-screens and computers. Front-Screen Projection was the method of having real foregrounds but projected images on wide screens for distant shots that appeared expansive. Scenes had to be 'stitched' together and we can view the lines. Clearly, Kubrick's cinematographic fingerprints can be seen in nearly every Apollo image.

Also, Kubrick created pinholes to the black backdrops in order to film stars. I immediately thought of scenes in *Star Trek Next Generation*. When they show the movements of star fields out of the windows, the process was done with holes in black sheets. Sorry to break trekker's hearts, but Gene Roddenberry was a 33 degree Freemason. That fact explains various Masonic inclusions throughout *Star Trek*.

The most convincing snippet of filmed Moon landing is during the scene where supposedly Armstrong is stepping off the LEM in that famous moment where he would be first touching the Moon. *LOOK WHAT HAPPENS...A BACKGROUND LIGHTING FIXTURE FALLS WITH A FLASH EXPLOSION OF THE LIGHTS...oops!* Look closely; this was not photo-shopped. The accident happened and was caught on film.

There are many visual discrepancies in the black, starless, lunar skies on all the moon landing footage. There is no doubt that these were "blacked-out" lunar skies, that were in reality scaffolding with breaks in seams of the F.S.P. screen employed by Kubrick.

Eyes Wide Shut is a 1999 film directed, produced, and co-written by Kubrick. He died four days after showing top executives at Warner Brothers his final cut of *Eyes Wide Shut*. The title of the film *Eyes Wide Shut* is an Illuminati term that means how most people go through life; *blind to what is directly in front of them in plain sight.* This film exposes what basically occurs and the horrendous acts performed in places of Secret Societies. The public controversy that swirled around *Eyes Wide Shut* concerned the sex-scenes that were added by computer technology to supposedly wipe out spots of graphic sex. We were misled again to not see the Rothschild influence in the film even to the point of

Kubrick using the Rothschild mansion and colors. People remain blind while their eyes are wide open. Relatively, only a few free-spirits have come to learn hidden (occult) truths and have the courage to talk about it openly.

I am convinced that all of the photos, films, and videotape of the Apollo Moon Missions are easily proven to be fake. Anyone with the slightest knowledge of photography, lighting, and physics can easily prove that NASA faked the visual records of the Apollo Space Program. As his reward, C. Fred Kleinknect, head of NASA at the time of the Apollo Space Program, is now the Sovereign Grand Commander of the Council of the 33rd Degree of the Ancient and Accepted Scottish Rite of Freemasonry of the Southern Jurisdiction.

As more and more people understand the revelations of the fraudulent nature of NASA and the Apollo space program by the

Central Intelligence Service and others, NASA has created a flood of propaganda, television programs, and films designed to keep the people trapped in their beliefs. The most ambitious are "Apollo 13" and "From the Earth to the Moon", both involving the actor/producer Tom Hanks. The latter opens with a monologue by Mr. Hanks who walks forward revealing a huge representation of the "God" Apollo (Sun, Osiris, lost word, etc.) guiding his chariot pulled by 4 horses through the heavens.

By now, I am sure that most readers are thinking that I should be wearing a tin foil hat. But I can say with conviction that no man has ever ascended higher than 300 miles, *if* that high, above the Earth's surface. No man has ever orbited, landed on, or walked upon the moon in any publicly known space program. If man has ever truly been to the moon it has been done in secret and with a far different technology than the one NASA claims to have used. I still remember viewing the photographs of cosmonauts in newspapers in my school library that had come back from high Earth orbits terribly burned by radiation, before such news was censored.

   The tremendous radiation encountered in the Van Allen Belt, solar radiation, cosmic radiation, temperature control, and many other problems connected with space travel prevent living organisms leaving our atmosphere with our known level of technology. Any intelligent high school student with a basic physics book can prove NASA faked the Apollo moon landings. If you doubt this, then please explain how the astronauts walked upon the moon's surface enclosed in a space suit in full sunlight absorbing a minimum of 265 degrees of heat surrounded by a vacuum. NASA tells us the moon has no atmosphere and that the astronauts were surrounded by the vacuum of space.

   Heat is defined as the vibration or movement of molecules within matter. The faster the molecular motion the higher the temperature. The slower the molecular motion the colder the temperature. Absolute zero is that point where all molecular motion ceases. In order to have hot or cold, molecules must be present.

A vacuum, and I'm not talking about the ones that you clean your carpets with, is a condition of nothingness where there are no molecules. Vacuums exist in degrees. Some scientists tell us that there is no such thing as an absolute vacuum. Space is the closest thing to an absolute vacuum that is known to us. There are so few molecules present in most areas of what we know as "space" that any concept of "hot" or "cold" is impossible to measure. A vacuum is a perfect insulator. That is why a "Thermos" or vacuum bottle is used to store hot or cold liquids, in order to maintain the temperature for the longest time possible without re-heating or re-cooling.

Radiation of all types will travel through a vacuum but will not affect the vacuum.

Radiant heat from the sun travels through the vacuum of space but does not "warm" space. In fact, the radiant heat of the sun has no effect whatsoever until it strikes matter. Molecular movement will increase in direct proportion to the radiant energy which is absorbed by matter. The time it takes to heat matter exposed to direct sunlight in space is determined by its color, its elemental properties, its distance from the sun, and its rate of absorption of radiant heat energy. Space is NOT hot. Space is NOT cold.

    Objects which are heated cannot be cooled by space. For an object to be able to cool it must first be removed from direct sunlight. Objects which are in the shadow of another object will eventually cool but not because space is "cold". Space is not cold. Hot and cold do not exist in the vacuum of space. Objects cool because the laws of motion dictate that the molecules of the object will slow down due to the resistance resulting from striking other molecules until eventually all motion will stop provided the object is sheltered from the direct and/or indirect radiation of the sun and that there is no other source of heat. Since the vacuum of space is the perfect insulator objects take a very long time to cool even when removed from all sources of heat, radiated or otherwise.

NASA insists that the space suits the astronauts supposedly wore on the lunar surface were air conditioned. An air conditioner cannot, and will not work without a heat exchanger. A heat exchanger simply takes heat gathered in a medium such as Freon gas from one place and transfers it to another place. This requires a medium of molecules which can absorb and transfer the heat such as an atmosphere or water. An air conditioner will not and cannot work in a vacuum. A space suit surrounded by a vacuum cannot transfer heat from the inside of the suit to any other place. The vacuum, remember, is a perfect insulator. A man would roast in his suit in such circumstances.

NASA also claims that the spacesuits were cooled by a water system which was piped around the body, then through a system of coils sheltered from the sun in the backpack. NASA claims that water was sprayed on the coils causing a coating of ice to form. The ice then supposedly absorbed the tremendous heat collected in the water and evaporated into space. There are two problems with this that cannot be explained away. 1) The amount of water needed to be carried by the astronauts to make this work for even a very small length of time in the direct 55° over the boiling point of water (210°F at sea level on Earth) heat of the sun could not have possibly been carried by the astronauts. 2) NASA has since claimed that they found ice in moon craters. NASA claims that ice sheltered from the direct rays of the sun will NOT evaporate, destroying their own bogus "air conditioning" explanation.

Remember this. Think about it the next

time you go off in the morning with a "vacuum bottle" filled with a piping hot Irish Coffee. Think about it long and hard when you sit down and pour a piping hot cup from your thermos to drink about four hours later. . . and then think about it again when you pour the last still very warm cup of Irish Coffee at the end of the day... if you haven't passed out yet.

The same laws of physics apply to any vehicle traveling through space. NASA claims that the spacecraft was slowly rotated causing the shadowed side to be cooled by the intense cold of space. . . an intense cold that DOES NOT EXIST. In fact, the only thing that could have been accomplished by a rotation of the spacecraft is a more even and constant heating such as that obtained by rotating a hot dog on a spit.

NASA knows better than to claim, in addition, that a water cooling apparatus such as that which they claim cooled the astronaut's suits was also used to cool the spacecraft. No rocket could ever have been launched with the amount of water needed to work such a system for even a very short period of time. Fresh water weighs a little over 62 lbs. per cubic foot. Space and weight capacity were critical given the lift capability of the rockets used in the Apollo Space Program. No such extra water was carried by any mission whatsoever for suits or for cooling the spacecraft.

On the tapes the Astronauts complained bitterly of the cold during their journey and while on the surface of the moon. They spoke of using heaters that did not give off enough heat to overcome the intense cold of space. It was imperative that NASA use this ruse because to tell the truth would TELL THE TRUTH. It is also proof of the arrogance and contempt in which the Illuminati holds over the common man.

NASA also claims that the space suits worn by the astronauts were pressurized at

5 psi over the ambient pressure (0 psi vacuum) on the moon's surface. The gloves NASA claims that the astronauts wore were made of pliable material containing no mechanical, hydraulic, or electrical devices which would aid the astronauts in the dexterous use of their fingers and hands while wearing the gloves. Experiments prove absolutely that such gloves are impossible to use and that the wearer cannot bend the wrist or fingers to do any dexterous work whatsoever when filled with 5 psi over ambient pressure either in a vacuum or in the earth's atmosphere. NASA showed on both film and television footage the astronauts using their hands and fingers normally during their trips to the so-called lunar surface. The films then clearly show that there is no pressure whatsoever within the gloves . . . a condition that would have caused explosive decompression of the astronauts resulting in almost immediate death if they had really been surrounded by the vacuum of space.

I want to believe, really, I do. But evidence suggests that NASA and the Apollo Space Program are two of the biggest lies ever foisted upon the unsuspecting and trusting citizens.

"There is nothing noble in being superior to your fellow man. True nobility lies in being superior to your former self."

-Ernest Hemingway

Chapter 11 *The Moon Is Made Out Of Cheese*

Every pre-conceived crime has a motive, and although I have already talked about motive throughout this book, there is one more that I would like to thoroughly bring to light, and that is money.

If you look at a crime and want to solve it, the best place to look is money. Who made out on the deal? Who stood to benefit?

Let's take 9/11 for example which was without a doubt a crime against the people of the United States as well as a crime against humanity. The biggest benefactor of 9/11 was what is known as the military industrial complex.

The military industrial complex is an informal alliance between a nation's military and the arms industry which supplies it, seen together as a vested interest which influences public policy. A driving factor behind this relationship between the government and defense-minded corporations is that both sides benefit--one side from obtaining war weapons, and the other from being paid to supply them.

In a present-day context, here in the United States, the appellation given to it sometimes is extended to military–industrial–congressional complex, adding the U.S. Congress to form a three-sided relationship termed an iron triangle (note: triangles are extremely symbolic in masonic symbolism).

These relationships include political contributions, taxpayer dollars, political approval for military spending, lobbying to support bureaucracies, and oversight of the industry; or more broadly to include the entire network of contracts and flows of money and resources among individuals as well as corporations and institutions of the defense contractors, private military contractors, The Pentagon, the Congress, and executive branches.

President of the United States Dwight D. Eisenhower used the term military industrial complex in his Farewell Address to the Nation on January 17, 1961:

A vital element in keeping the peace is our military establishment. Our arms must be mighty, ready for instant action, so that no potential aggressor may be tempted to risk his own destruction...

"This conjunction of an immense military establishment and a large arms industry is new in the American experience. The total influence—economic, political, even spiritual—is felt in every city, every statehouse, every office of the federal government. We recognize the imperative need for this development. Yet we must not fail to comprehend its grave implications. Our toil, resources and livelihood are all involved; so is the very structure of our society. In the councils of government, we must guard against the acquisition of unwarranted influence, whether sought or unsought, by the military–industrial complex. The potential for the disastrous rise of misplaced power exists, and will persist. We must never let the weight of this combination endanger our liberties or democratic processes. We should take nothing for granted. Only an alert and knowledgeable citizenry can compel the proper meshing of the huge industrial and military machinery of defense with our peaceful methods and goals so that security and liberty may prosper together."

Unfortunately, Eisenhower's warning was too late.

The Apollo program cost $20 billion in then-year dollars, $30 billion in 1970s dollars, or $115 billion in today's money. So, let's just say for example that Apollo never went to the moon. Then what might have happened to the $115 billion of taxpayer dollars that the program cost?

On March 23, 1983, President Reagan proposed the creation of the Strategic Defense Initiative (SDI), an ambitious project that would construct a space-based anti-missile system. This program was immediately dubbed "Star Wars", named after the popular 1977 film by George Lucas and Disney. Yep, Disney's name sure does come up a lot.

The SDI was intended to defend the United States from attack from Soviet ICBMs by intercepting the missiles at various phases of their flight. For the interception, the SDI would require extremely advanced technological systems, yet to be researched and developed. Among the potential components of the defense system were both space- and earth-based laser battle stations, which, by a combination of methods, would direct their killing beams toward moving Soviet targets. Air-based missile platforms and ground-based missiles using other non-nuclear killing mechanisms would constitute the rear echelon of defense and would be concentrated around such major targets as U.S. ICBM silos. The sensors to detect attacks would be based on the ground, in the air, and in space, and would use radar, optical, and infrared threat-detection systems.

   This system would tip the nuclear balance toward the United States. The Soviets feared that SDI would enable the United States to launch a first-strike against them. Critics pointed to the vast technological uncertainties of the system, in addition to its enormous cost.

   Although work was begun on the program, the technology proved to be too complex and much of the research was cancelled by later administrations. The idea of missile defense system would resurface later as the National Missile Defense.

The United States spends more than the next seven countries combined on defense. In 2014, the most recent year available, the United States led the world in military spending at $610 billion, marking 34 percent of the world total. If that seems like a huge number, it's because it is and that number doesn't include the money that is covertly diverted from other programs to defense.

This defense budget is more than the combined military spending of China, Russia, the United Kingdom, Japan, France, Saudi Arabia, India, Germany, Italy and Brazil.

It is likely that nearly all Americans hate the idea of their tax dollars being spent to enrich corporations; especially when those very same corporations control where Americans' tax dollars are spent. It is not enough that the 2015-16 budget allotted well over 60 percent of all *"on the book"* government spending to the military; if a bevy of defense contractor lobbies have their way Americans will likely see the lion's share of their tax dollars going directly to the military industrial complex. It has become the great beast that hungers for more and more.

It is safe to say that the majority of Americans do not oppose a portion of their tax dollars going to defense; the county's security is the one expense that few Americans oppose. However, the nation should not exist to profit the military industrial complex.

The citizens of this country deserve more than to work just to support the defense industry. They deserve decent schools, hospitals, highways, bridges, and domestic programs that any sane human being would regard as necessary for *"the general welfare of the people."* But this is America and with a robust propaganda campaign to keep Americans terrified, they are able to continually suck more and more money from the veins of the taxpayer.

Eisenhower warned that "an immense military establishment and a large arms industry" had emerged as a hidden force in US politics and that Americans "must not fail to comprehend its grave implications". The speech may have been Eisenhower's most courageous and prophetic moment. Fifty years and some later, Americans find themselves in what seems like perpetual war. No sooner do we draw down on operations in Iraq than leaders demand an intervention in Libya or Syria or Iran. While perpetual war constitutes perpetual losses for families, and ever expanding budgets, it also represents perpetual profits for a new and larger complex of business and government interests.

The new military-industrial complex is fueled by a conveniently ambiguous and unseen enemy: the terrorist. Former President George W. Bush and his aides insisted on calling counter-terrorism efforts a "war".

While few politicians are willing to admit it, we don't just endure wars we seem to need war - at least for some people. A study showed that roughly 75 percent of the fallen in these wars come from working class families. They do not need war. They pay the cost of the war.

Military and homeland budgets now support millions of people in an otherwise declining economy. Hundreds of billions of dollars flow each year from the public coffers to agencies and contractors who have an incentive to keep the country on a war-footing - and footing the bill for war.

In the last eight years, trillions of dollars have flowed to military and homeland security companies. When the administration starts a war like Libya, it is a windfall for companies who are given generous contracts to produce everything from replacement missiles to ready-to-eat meals. And there are thousands of lobbyists in Washington to guarantee the ever-expanding budgets for war and homeland security.

The National Aeronautics and Space Administration (NASA) is an independent agency of the executive branch of the United States government responsible for the civilian space program as well as aeronautics and aerospace research.

President Eisenhower established NASA in 1958 with a distinctly civilian (rather than military) orientation encouraging peaceful applications in space science...which wouldn't last a day.

Furnishing cover stories for covert operations, monitoring Soviet missile tests, and supplying weather data to the U.S. military have been part of the secret side of NASA since its inception in 1958, according to declassified documents.

Even though Congress's intention in forming NASA was to establish a purely civilian space agency, a combination of circumstances led the agency to commingle its activities with black programs operated by the U.S. military and Intelligence Community.

Even before NASA formally began operations in October 1958, the CIA offered its leadership Office of Scientific Intelligence reports and briefings on the Soviet space program. Access to this information was quickly given to selected working-level officials. National Intelligence Estimates (NIEs) and Special National Intelligence Estimates (SNIEs) published by the U.S. Intelligence Board were the highest-level reports on the Soviet space program and other issues.

The CIA established the Foreign Missile and Space Analysis Center (FMSAC) in 1963 as the primary office to analyze all foreign space and missile programs. It produced a wide range of publications (including some on a daily or weekly basis) and conducted briefings of CIA, NASA, and other officials.

By 1966, NASA's leadership was receiving both FMSAC's publications and regular briefings by its personnel on the Soviet space program. NASA continues to receive intelligence reports and briefings into today.

Let me just mention a couple of examples of the military-industrial complex/NASA connection such as NASA's space shuttle putting military satellites into orbit and other military tests that are done on-board the Space Station.

In July 2009, NASA indicated that it must have erased the original Apollo 11 Moon footage years ago so that it could re-use the tape. Just imagine erasing the tapes of man's greatest achievement. But it wasn't just one tape. In December 2009, NASA issued a final report on the Apollo 11 telemetry tapes. After a three-year search, the "inescapable conclusion" was that about 45 tapes (estimated 15 tapes recorded at each of the three tracking stations) of Apollo 11 video were erased and re-used. I would have to say that to make a mistake once by erasing even one tape is suspicious. To erase all 45 smells like fish laying on a sidewalk, in Phoenix, in the summertime, and for a day.

It smells like NASA's Apollo program might have been a way to divert taxpayer money to something entirely different than landing on the Moon.

For centuries, scientists have wrestled to explain the origin of the Moon. Popular theories include a giant impact event (in which a Mars-sized object collided with Earth and ejected debris formed the Moon), Earth rapidly spinning such that a part of the crust flew into space, Earth capturing a body floating from the solar system, and the Moon and Earth forming from the solar nebula as a double system. However, analysis of the rocks astronauts brought back from the Moon casts doubt on all those models and suggests a better model where the Moon is made out of cheese.

"All men have crimes, and most of them are hidden."

-Anonymous

Chapter 12 *Catching A Buzz*

Buzz Aldrin, former astronaut and supposedly the second person to walk on the moon, was harassed in Los Angeles by a man who claims NASA faked the six manned lunar landings.

Videographer Bart Sibrel, 37, poked Aldrin with a Bible, demanding that the then 72-year-old swear he really walked on the moon. He also called Aldrin a thief, liar and coward. Aldrin punched him in the face.

Now NASA, with the help of a local author, journalist and Mission Control veteran, is planning to land a punch of its own.

James Oberg, a 22-year Mission Control veteran, is at work to try to debunk the theories of those who claim NASA faked the six manned lunar landings, it will also examine how such theories take hold, gain popularity and spread.

Oberg, author of 12 space-related books and a regular contributor to ABC News, said he'd lobbied to do the research for years.

Half the world's population wasn't yet born the last time an American walked on the moon, and as more time passes, the less real the lunar missions seem. As time progresses, this gets less and less real to everybody.

It's not just a few crackpots and their new books and Internet conspiracy sites, but there are entire subcultures within the U.S., and substantial cultures around the world, that strongly believe the landings were faked. This is official dogma still taught in schools in Cuba, plus wherever else Cuban teachers have been sent (such as Nicaragua and Angola).

Let's examine claims that lunar photographs and video transmission from

1969 are full of inconsistencies. People who are puzzled by something deserve an attempt at an explanation.

Let's start with the photos. Let's discuss the stars in NASA's photos:

NASA claims the pictures taken on the Apollo missions is proof positive that they landed men on the moon. This is Photography 101. The Apollo astronauts were using several types of cameras to record their lunar adventures, one being modified medium-format Hasselblad 500 EL cameras mounted to their spacesuits. These were film cameras and had to be set just right to get pictures to develop correctly—not unlike today's digital cameras, but without the convenience of auto mode! All the astronauts went through training on how to shoot with the cameras, so when they got to the Moon they were able to take some really great shots of the surface in beautiful 70mm detail.

Having discussed earlier the pin points in the black background to create stars, and the non-use of their fingers because of the gloves they were wearing, NASA's rebuttal does not hold up.

When asked why you can still see objects in the shadows of the photographs and isn't this a sign of a different light source on the moon photos NASA had this to say.

It's true that light on Earth is scattered by the atmosphere, and so we can see even where sunlight isn't directly illuminating a scene. And in space, shadows can be incredibly dark because of the lack of this effect. But there is still reflected light, and *the lunar surface is reflective.*

They claim that this is the result of reflected light from the Sun hitting the lunar regolith and bouncing back up into the shadows, not "another source of artificial illumination" claimed by some conspiracy believers.

I believe that many of the moon's images were shot by using NASA's lunar orbiter. The Lunar Orbiter program was a series of five unmanned lunar orbiter missions launched by the United States from 1966 through 1967. Which NASA claims was Intended to help select Apollo landing sites by mapping the Moon's surface. They provided the first photographs from lunar orbit.

If you have noticed the images of the astronauts in their suits on the moon, you will notice that their cameras are not protected from the radiation on the moon's surface. If you were around in the days before digital cameras and ever went through airport security and forgot to take the film out of your 35mm camera, chances are you would lose every image on that film...and the radiation from an airport x-ray is nowhere near that of deep space.

Airports use x-ray equipment to scan checked and carry-on baggage. Film can tolerate some x-ray exposure but excessive amounts result in objectionable fog (an increase in base film density and a noticeable increase in grain). The faster the film the greater the effects of the x-rays.

That film would have been exposed to hour after hour of constant radiation and intense heat.

The Hasselblad camera had to work in the extreme conditions of space, with vacuum and temperatures varying from 120° C in the sun to minus 65° C in shadow. The camera was painted silver to make it more resistant to the variations in temperature. Conventional lubricants had to be eliminated as they would boil off in the vacuum of space.

When on the lunar surface, the camera was mounted on a bracket on the chest of the astronaut's space suit. This both provided some support to the camera, and made it possible to manipulate the rings and levers with both hands. A trigger was fitted under the camera to make it easier to fire. But what about that psi in the gloves?

The cameras did not even have any light metering or automatic exposure. Based on experimentation on earlier Apollo missions, NASA says exposure settings for the different kinds of expected lighting conditions were worked out in advance.

I've shot film in almost any different lighting condition imaginable and basically without a light meter you pretty much are guessing at what is going to come out. The 500 EL Data Cameras did not have a viewfinder either, as the astronaut's helmets restricted their movement too much for it to be useful. Instead the lens was fitted with a simple sight that the astronauts used to point the camera in the right direction. This is of course not a very accurate method. I am extremely skeptical about this. Even in the controlled environment of a photo studio, with no light meter, and no viewfinder, and no finger dexterity to manipulate the camera's settings, the photographic results would be non-usable.

NASA says a total of 1407 exposures were made during the Apollo 11 mission, on 9 magazines of film. 857 black & white photos and 550 color photos. Only the film magazines were brought back from the moon. 12 Hasselblad cameras were left behind on the lunar surface during the Apollo program.

Supposedly the magazines were loaded with a special-designed film NASA contracted Kodak to develop. For black and white they used 70mm perforated Kodak Panatomic-X 'fine-grained' film with an ASA rating of 80. For color, they could've used any combination of Kodak Ektachrome SO–68, Kodak Ektachrome SO–121, and Kodak 2485, the latter of which featured a 'super light-sensitive' ASA rating of 1,600.

Film suffers the effects of ambient gamma radiation. Video tape is even worse.

Naturally occurring gamma radiation increases the D-min and toe densities and also increases grain. Higher speed films are affected more by gamma radiation than lower speed films. A camera film with an EI (Exposure Index) of 800 has a much greater change than an EI 200 film. Exposed and unprocessed film that has been properly refrigerated retains the speed and contrast of the exposure conditions, but the overall D-min, toe and grain will continue to increase over time and when exposed to heat.

Still, NASA says the pictures shot on the surface of the moon have changed the way we view the universe and our part in it. They have made us feel small, made us feel large, and made us feel bound to one another as humans.

These photographs have enabled the average person to understand, in the blink of an eye, relationships which were previously the reserve of a tiny minority of experts. These images demand no previous knowledge, they don't disqualify all the millions of people in the world who cannot read, they are equally accessible to any and all who can see.

The beauty of these photos works intuitively and almost instantly. We see a picture of Earth, for instance, poised like a blue-green jewel against the black of space, we see its surprisingly thin layer of atmosphere, we look upon the whole of our planet and are struck by how delicate and small it appears.

When you look at the number of photographs taken by astronauts during all Apollo missions and divided this by the duration of their time spent on the moon, you arrives at a figure of 1.19 photos shot per minute by the astronauts. That is one photo per 50 seconds. Discounting time spent on other activities, such as planting the flag in the ground, walking time, etc., this results in one photo taken every 15 seconds for Apollo 11. This of course, is simply impossible. What is even more remarkable because many places in the photographs are miles apart and would have taken considerable travel time to reach, especially in bulky pressure suits. And remember, the cameras were equipped with neither a viewfinder nor an automatic exposure control, so taking the pictures would have taken considerably longer. How much longer? Again, in the controlled environment of a photo studio using the same Hasselblad camera with the added convenience of a light meter, each photo that we would shoot (without bulky gloves with 5 psi on our hands), would take approximately one and a half minutes. That is with no other time spent doing other tasks. If one phot is faked, then all must be assumed to be faked.

> *"My first words of my impression of being on the surface of the Moon that just came to my mind was "Magnificent desolation."*
> *The magnificence of human beings, humanity, Planet Earth, maturing the*

technologies, imagination and courage to expand our capabilities beyond the next ocean, to dream about being on the Moon, and then taking advantage of increases in technology and carrying out that dream — achieving that is magnificent testimony to humanity. But it is also desolate — there is no place on earth as desolate as what I was viewing in those first moments on the Lunar Surface.

Because I realized what I was looking at, towards the horizon and in every direction, had not changed in hundreds, thousands of years. Beyond me I could see the moon curving away — no atmosphere, black sky. Cold.

Colder than anyone could experience on Earth when the sun is up- but when the sun is up for 14 days, it gets very, very hot. No sign of life whatsoever.

That is desolate. More desolate than any place on Earth."

~ Buzz Aldrin, Apollo 11 and 2nd man to allegedly walk on the Moon.

Moon temperatures make it Impossible to be on the Moon, much less truck around on Moon buggies, touch hotter than hell moon rocks and set up sensor equipment.

Yet everything, always worked great, we are told, even though man had never, ever experienced such temperatures on Earth. Radio communications, sensors, mobile devices, coolant systems, batteries, buggies, fuel, and especially photographic equipment had no problem.

Due to no atmosphere, the temperatures range each day on the sunny side of the moon from a minus 387 F degrees to a plus 225 F. The space suits, just millimeters thick and so flexible they creased, keep cooled, no worries. Besides having to carry gallons and gallons of water in their packs to run their inner A/C along with batteries, oxygen and human waste tubes and reservoirs.

Just at the time digital imaging was taking apart the NASA photos, they went lost. *The missing tapes were among over 700 boxes of magnetic data tapes recorded throughout the Apollo program which have not been found. On August 16, 2006 NASA announced its official search saying, "The original tapes may be at the Goddard Space Flight Center ... or at another location within the NASA archiving system. NASA engineers are hopeful that when the tapes are found they can use today's digital technology to provide a version of the moonwalk that is much better quality than what we have today."*

Ninety five percent of NASA's Moon pictures on their web sites, were never seen before the internet was launched. My assumption is that they had to produce a considerable number of fake Moon pictures, for all six missions, otherwise the public would want to know why there were so few. Not all of NASA's fake Apollo pictures have been altered with Photoshop. The main Apollo 11 picture of Buzz Aldrin, as well press released pictures from Apollo 12 and Apollo 14 showing astronauts holding the flag were most probably taken in the fake Moonscape at Langley Research Center, and did not require any alteration to pass off as a Moon photographs.

It would be easy to assume that all the fake Moon stills and video were shot in a remote studio in the Nevada desert somewhere, but I don't think that this is the case. Both video and still shots were probably taken at many different places, and the actual videos were most probably shot in remote desert locations many years before the actual mission dates. One of the places chosen by NASA and the USGS, was Chezhin Chotah in the Hopi Butte volcanic field. The USGS (United States Geological Society) were heavily involved in assisting NASA to perfect the fake Moon scenario's, as a direct result of them being funded by none other than NASA. Being that many of these were shot before the actual missions, then the planning and preparation of faking the Moon missions began way back in the early 1960's.

I have always been attracted to the odd and the curious. Growing up in a small town, I paid admission to countless magic, hypnotism, and spook shows, not to mention the juggling acts, that played in the school auditorium. And I must have attended every carnival or circus that came around.

A major type of sideshow, often popularly called a "freak show," since human oddities were usually among the exhibits, was known to insider "carnys" as a "ten-in-one." As its name indicated, it consisted of a number of acts, often arrayed along a platform, with the crowd moving from one to the other in sequence. Since such shows were typically continuous, if a spectator entered the tent during, say, the sword swallower's performance, he or she would be led by the "lecturer" through the remaining nine (approximately) acts or features-magician, fat lady, giant, etc.- and when the sword swallower was on again, that was the signal to exit the show.

  At the end of each act or exhibit spectators might be offered a pitched item such as a "true life" booklet or photograph. Another type of sideshow features is represented by what is known as an "illusion show." An example-as old as it is effective, is a transformation effect such as girl-to-gorilla, skeletal-corpse-to-living-vampire, etc.

While attending Pennsylvania's Clearfield County Fair, I was drawn to a show that had a large photograph of a two-headed cow outside. I paid my admission and entered the tent only to find three men in a two-headed cow costume. They did not lie. After all, I was told I would see a two-headed cow inside and I did. Often a spectator would ask of an exhibit, "Is it real?" The answer from carny's everywhere: "Oh, it's all real."

Virtually every game along the midway of a carnival has the potential for being rigged, yet few individuals outside the midway are familiar enough with the games to recognize one that is total chance or a crooked one. Because of this, Carnies operate with little fear of retaliation. Carnivals are not "nickel and dime" operations as most people believe.

Billions of dollars per year are spent at carnivals.

  In the film "The Prestige", based upon the novel by Christopher Priest, they say: "Every great magic trick consists of three parts or acts. The first part is called "The Pledge". The magician shows you something ordinary: a deck of cards, a bird or a man. He shows you this object. Perhaps he asks you to inspect it to see if it is indeed real, unaltered, normal. But of course, it probably isn't. The second act is called "The Turn". The magician takes the ordinary something and makes it do something extraordinary. Now you're looking for the secret... but you won't find it, because of course you're not really looking. You don't really want to know. You want to be fooled. But you wouldn't clap yet. Because making something disappear isn't enough; you have to bring it back. That's why every magic trick has a third act, the hardest part, the part we call "The Prestige"."

Why do people want to be cheated and watch these tricks?

To most people, it would be considered harmless entertainment. Being fooled by a magician is just fun because it creates the illusion that the impossible is possible. When you find out the secret behind the trick that illusion is lost and it isn't fun anymore. The real problem starts when people allow this type of thinking to extend to other areas such as believing sales advertisements, politicians, and other less scrupulous types.

Not so many people love to be fooled as much as they simply do not like to think hard. One of the biggest travesties to watch is people who are very opinionated, yet closed minded. They like to be in the leader seat but have not engaged in the act of thinking.

This applies to The Prestige because people are not looking to be fooled, they are looking to have someone hand the answer, the entertainment, and the gratification to them on a platter.

"You can't make the same mistake twice. The second time you make it, it's no longer a mistake. It's a choice."

-Anonymous

Chapter 13 *Capitalism*

In the United States, everything is monetized. Everything from speculation on when you will die by insurance companies and wall street traders to the value of one single ear of corn.

A federal court set the value of the moon rocks at $50,800 per gram based on how much it cost the U.S. government to retrieve the samples between 1969 and 1972. At $50,800 per gram, the value of a moon rock is much more than the value of a diamond. Yet, NASA claims to not know the location of most of the moon rocks.

One can only surmise that by 2017, women would be wearing moon rock rings with the highly-polished stones set into well-crafted gold or platinum settings by world respected jewelers. But they are not. People would be lining up for their moon trip, and although not cheap, it would be a most sought after experience for the world's elite. According to a recent Gallup poll, about a fourth of the United States population -- 27% -- say they would like to go to the moon.

Civilizations, for good reasons, have an idea of some of the things that are part of nature's bounty that money ought not be able to buy. Forests, rivers, sanctity of the human body, blood, water, are some of the things that civilizational wisdom recommends that we should protect from monetization. Citizens' votes should not be bought and sold, for good reasons related to the ideal of self-rule and democracy.

The modern trend to monetize everything ignores civilizational wisdom.

This trend has been carried forward the furthest in the United States.

Too many people believe everything fed to them by the media, but to be honest, how can they really know? They take it on faith that the news and academia wouldn't lie to them. That's what leads them to thinking we're nuts. Conspiracy theories are disregarded and mocked with impunity. According to the media, those who believe in such notions have mental defects.

Back to 2001, Fox Network aired the documentary "Conspiracy Theory: Did We Land on the Moon?" This film presented multiple aspects and accounts as evidence that NASA faked the lunar landings. To the casual viewer, the documentary likely came across as convincing, and to those who don't go for conspiracies, they probably dismissed it as poppycock conspiracy.

Once the documentary had aired was when the Illuminati went to work. The order's so-called "rational" sources such as the Discovery Channel, National Geographic, CNN, and countless others immediately moved to debunk the film's claims. Needless to say, they succeeded. From the shadows in the photographs to the "waving" flag, the Illuminati's henchmen quickly made believing in such preposterous notions ridiculous.

The real evidence for NASA faking the moon landings isn't found in shadows, it's found in NASA's recent research. The latest findings on the toxicity of radiation in deep space combined with the fact that officials continue alluding to the truth that the technology to get to the moon still isn't available is the actual proof. The Illuminati hopes that you won't or even be motivated to find it if you consider the whole Apollo hoax theory to be lies and ignorance.

In 1968 NASA Chief Astronaut, Deke Slayton, (one of the main perpetrators of faking Apollo), visited the film set of "2001 Space Odyssey", in the UK He referred to it as NASA East, and it was here that he got the idea for filming the mock lunar module, and command module separation and docking. Film of the alleged booster stage falling away from module was also sequenced on Kubrick's film set. Think about it, how could you install a camera in the center part of a rocket booster engine without it being burned to a crisp? It can only be done on a film set, and why is it we only see this sequence, albeit repeated for each Apollo mission, only on the Moon missions, and not on any other space mission? TV pictures allegedly beamed back to Earth showing the lunar module separation, were razor sharp color images, why therefore were the TV transmissions from the Moon gray and fuzzy, after all they were supposedly transmitted across the same distance in space?

Many point to President Richard Nixon as the main culprit behind one of the biggest lies ever inflicted on society. This however is incorrect because the idea's and planning which went into faking the Moon missions began in the early 60's, following Kennedy's now infamous speech to Congress. It was therefore L B Johnson who had the most inside knowledge and plans to fake the Moon mission, and it was he who made most of the Apollo material classified, with a declassification date of 2026.

Nixon took office shortly before Apollo 11, but continued the lies under guidance from the CIA in-order-to boost American pride which was at the time at an all-time low. Every US President from L B J up to today are fully aware that the Moon missions were faked, but the CIA have the upper hand when it comes to American security, and how space pride can alter a population.

In 1981, long time skeptic of the Apollo Moon missions, Bill Kaysing appeared on the Oprah Winfrey show, detailing how NASA had conned the American people into believing that they had landed men on the Moon. A national survey at the time by the program makers showed a staggering 60% of Americans believed the Moon landings were faked. About 7 out of 10 Americans who are 35 years of age or older say they watched the moon landing on television in July, 1969, so 60% was a staggering number.

It appears that some of the hyperbole surrounding the moon effort is not necessarily endorsed by the average American. A July 13-14 poll asked Americans if they agreed with a statement, based on an assertion appearing on the NASA web site, that "the human race accomplished its single greatest technological achievement of all time by landing a man on the moon." Only 39% agree with this statement. Fifty-nine percent don't.

In July 20th 2016 more than half of British adults claimed that the Apollo 11 mission was fake.

The astonishing revelation that 52% of people in the UK believe that Neil Armstrong's *one small step for man, one giant leap for mankind* speech was recorded somewhere on Earth.

Then again, people are also more inclined to believe in the existence of ghosts and spirits than God (30% vs 29%).

Could it be that conspiracy theories are not just the implausible visions of a paranoid minority? A national poll released reported that 37 percent of Americans believe that global warming is a hoax, 21 percent think that the US government is covering up evidence of alien existence and 28 percent believe a secret elite power with a globalist agenda is conspiring to rule the world.

There is an old saying that "A liar needs a good memory". Nowhere is this more-true than in the Apollo program. NASA tell lies to cover up previous lies, and other discrepancies uncovered by people investigating the Moon landings. Altering previous data, removing photographs, and retracting statements made, only re-enforces the evidence that NASA are on the run, and being forced into a corner to which they cannot escape. The actions of those under investigation makes the investigator more aware they are bluffing. The longer that person, or persons, who make the extravagant claims continue, the more lies they have to tell in order to counteract it, until it reaches the point where it becomes ridiculous. That point was passed in July 1999, when NASA officials were questioned about the Moon landings on television. They dodged the all-important questions like a drifter dodges the heat.

In a recent poll in 2016, one in two people surveyed had doubts about the Government's account of 9/11. 38% of Americans have some doubts about the official account of 9/11, 10% do not believe it at all, and 12% are unsure about it

After viewing video footage of World Trade Center Building 7's collapse, 46% suspect that it was caused by a controlled demolition. Building 7, a 47-story skyscraper, collapsed into its own footprint late in the afternoon on 9/11.

"Even the government's own computer model disproves its theory. It looks nothing like the actual collapse," said Tony Szamboti, *a mechanical engineer from the Philadelphia area. "Not only that, they*

refuse to release the data that would allow us to verify their model. In the world of science, this is as bad as it gets. I'm glad most people can look at the collapse and see the obvious."

Apparently, a monumental shift is in process that most have not recognized yet. The truth, or at least some truth, is about to be shown to the American masses about 9/11. I say American masses because almost everyone knows that the US government conspiracy theory on 9/11 is for people with tinfoil hats that are either completely zombified or are under mass hypnosis. Most of the rest of the world looks on the US like "The Truman Show" and can't believe how many people in the show don't realize it's not real.

During the past 15 years, I have not met a single individual who, after doing research on the subject, switched from questioning the official narrative of the events of 9/11/2001 to believing the official narrative of those events.

Fifteen years have passed since the infamous events of September 11th, 2001 took place, and the majority of people still don't know a damn thing about the actual details of that event. They don't know what was going on in the country with regard to our military that day. They don't know the history or the activities of key members of our government, defense establishment or intelligence community, on, or during the weeks, and in some cases the years leading up to that day. They don't know what took place during or immediately following the events of that day. And they don't know what actions were taken by those key people following that event.

NASA claims that man-made objects are still on the moon and transmissions came *from* the moon, and that there is no "faking" this. They claim this is proof conclusive than man walked on the moon. But again, there are also Soviet objects on the moon, and transmissions could easily have been made through bouncing a signal off an antenna there from a piece of equipment, just as easily as a transmission could have been faked from Earth. A Google search this week for "Apollo moon landing hoax" can yield more than 1.5 billion results.

We had Apollo in 1969. The Shuttle in 1981. Nothing in 2011. Our space program would look awesome to anyone living backwards through time.

The 1979 Moon Treaty (Article 11) declares that 'the Moon and its natural resources are the common heritage of mankind' and ban any state, corporate or private individual ownership of them. Since this treaty was not signed by the US or by any other country likely to send a mission to the Moon this clause was without effect. Note the article number. Yes, it's 11.

Venture capital firms invested $1.8 billion in commercial space startups in 2015, nearly doubling the amount of venture cash invested in the industry in all of the previous 15 years combined. Venture capital firms are now piling money into young space companies with unprecedented gusto, however that funding is primarily for satellite technologies and are not related to deep space research.

NASA has a larger budget than nearly all the world's civilian space agencies, combined. It also has one of the U.S. federal government's biggest procurement budgets. Meanwhile, the price of sending U.S. astronauts into space has gone nowhere but up over the past several decades.

A Trip to the Moon is a 1902 French silent film directed by Georges Méliès. The film follows a group of astronomers who travel to the Moon in a cannon-propelled capsule, explore the Moon's surface, escape from an underground group of Selenites (lunar inhabitants), and return to Earth with no problems.

A Trip to the Moon combined "spectacle, sensation, and technical wizardry to create a cosmic fantasy that was an international sensation. It was profoundly influential on later filmmakers, bringing creativity to the cinematic medium and offering fantasy for pure entertainment, a rare goal in film at the time. In addition, Méliès's innovative editing and special effects techniques were widely imitated and became important elements of the medium. The film also spurred on the development of cinematic science fiction and fantasy by demonstrating that scientific themes worked on the screen and that reality could be transformed by the camera. You can sum up Méliès's importance to film history by commenting that Méliès "profoundly influenced the film industry and gave inspiration to a generation of viewers. His budget for the film was 10,000 French francs, or roughly $1613 and ninety-three cents.

"Thinking is hard work, which is why so few people engage in it."

-Albert Einstein

Chapter 15 *Skeletons in the closet*

For nearly two decades leading up to the signing of the Declaration of Independence Benjamin Franklin lived in London in a house at 36 Craven Street. In 1776, Franklin left his English home to come back to America. More than 200 years later, 15 bodies were found in the basement, buried in a secret, windowless room beneath the garden. At the time, nearly all the civil offices in the country were in the hands of Freemasons; and that the press was completely under their control.

Franklin was a noted revolutionary and powerful freemason— the Grand Master of Masons of Pennsylvania—so it's easy to wonder what dark secrets Franklin may have hidden in his basement chamber.

The mainstream media's explanation is not mass murder, but an anatomy school run by Benjamin Franklin's young friend and protege, William Hewson, which were still illegal studies.

Everyone knows how Benjamin Franklin flew his kite into a thunderstorm and proved lightning was actually just electricity. Most people believe Franklin made his shocking discovery in 1752 with the help of his son, William. Using a silk string so he wouldn't end up a "Fried Founding Father," Franklin sent an iron key up into the atmosphere—and the rest is history.

Word of Franklin's success spread around the globe and eventually inspired an Italian physiologist named Luigi Galvani. Thanks to Franklin's experiments, Galvani started zapping a bunch of dead frogs to see what would happen. As it turns out, the electricity activated the amphibians' muscles, causing the legs to kick.

In turn, Galvani's research inspired showmen, who got their hands on human corpses and "awakened" the dead with electric current. These ghastly sideshows caught the attention of a young woman named Mary Shelley, who took Galvani's discovery and turned it into the world's most famous horror story *Frankenstein*. Some people even think the "Frank" in *Frankenstein* comes from Benjamin Franklin's last name.

In 1998, conservationists were doing repairs on 36 Craven, looking to turn Franklin's old haunt into a museum. From a one-meter wide, one-meter deep pit, over 1200 pieces of bone were retrieved.

Researchers think that 36 Craven was an irresistible spot for Hewson to establish his own anatomy lab. The tenant was a trusted friend, the landlady was his mother-in-law, and he was flanked by convenient sources for corpses. Bodies could be smuggled from graveyards and delivered to the wharf at one end of the street, or snatched from the gallows at the other end. When he was done with them, Hewson simply buried whatever was left of the bodies in the basement, rather than sneak them out for disposal elsewhere and risk getting caught and prosecuted for dissection and grave robbing.

Perhaps, the bones were a result of something far more sinister. Masonic organizations promote the idea that they are a force against religious extremism. The mainstream freemasonry descending from the United Grand Lodge of England requires that its members profess a belief in Deity, but does not inquire further about the specific details of their religious beliefs.

The lodges confer "degrees" of initiation on their members at ritual meetings.

During each conferral, the candidate is made to kneel at an altar and swear a blood oath whereby they promise to keep the secrets of the order, with violations of that oath being punishable by extreme physical mutilation. These punishments, which vary in specifics with each degree, are explicitly and graphically described to the candidate before he is asked to take the oath.

The Freemasons are the world's largest secret society with five million members (including three million Americans.) Only their inner circles are aware that the *Craft* is in fact devoted to Satanism.

Throughout history, many world leaders were masons. George W. Bush is a member. As a student at Yale Bush joined its "Skull and Bones" chapter and referred to it in August 2000 in these terms: "My heritage is part of who I am."

Dick Cheney and Colin Powell are also high level Freemasons. So is Al Gore and Ariel Sharon. Past Presidents FDR, Harry Truman, Ronald Reagan and Lyndon Johnson were also members. So are Henry Kissinger, Allen Greenspan and World Bank President James Wolfensohn.

And there is a dark side. Freemasonry has been blamed for many cases of child sexual abuse and ritual murder.

Looking at the United States and it ongoing involvement in war, one has to wonder why? In addition to oil, for example the war against Iraq is part of a long-term plan to establish the rule of Satan on earth. The New World Order is Masonic in character. Sadaam Hussein (and Islam in general) represent an obstacle to the Masonic plan to rebuild Solomon's Temple on the Temple Mount in Jerusalem. This will be the seat of a new world religion subtly devoted to Lucifer.

The endless wars are nothing but a step-by-step plan to enslave humanity. For example, the United Nations' true character is revealed by the fact that the only religious chapel at its headquarters is run by a satanic cult, the "Lucis Trust." The name was changed from Lucifer Trust to make the nature of the organization less conspicuous. I think anyone would agree that there are dangerous and diabolical folks making long-term plans to seize even more power and destroy any vestige of freedom left in the world.

Freemasonry is a pagan cult that pretends to embrace all religions in-order-to negate them all. It says there is no God but man. Man, not God is the measure of all things. Our lust for more power, money, and sex is unleashed. The lower instincts become the higher.

Communism has been the main instrument of the Illuminati. (The

Communist anniversary of May 1st refers to the date the Illuminati was founded in 1776.) The Protocols of the Elders of Zion was probably an Illuminati document disguised as a Jewish one. Certainly, Jews like Karl Marx and Leon Trotsky dominated Communism but they were Freemasons first. They did not represent the Jewish people.

It's easy to look back in history at Bolshevik Russia as a French Orient Masonic state. The slaughter of millions of Russians by the CHEKA was Masonic ritual murder. There numerous Masonic symbols carved into the flesh of victims' heads, faces, necks and torsos. The assassination of Czar Nicholas II and his family was also a Masonic ritual murder.

We don't hear much about the "holocaust" of educated Russians between 1918 and 1922. The Bolshevik Freemasons slaughtered 3,200,000 people. Husbands, fathers and brothers were compelled to watch as their wives, daughters and sisters were brutally raped.

Published in "The Scotsman" on November 7, 1923 are the following counts of the slaughtered to bring about the Craft's "dictatorship of the proletariat":

"28 bishops, 1219 priests, 6000 professors and teachers, 9000 doctors, 54,000 officers, 260,000 soldiers, 70,000 policemen, 12,950 property owners, 535,250 members of the intellectual and liberal professions, 193,290 workmen, 618,000 peasants."

It's even possible that the Second World War was essentially a civil war between two branches of Freemasonry. The English Grand Lodge built up Adolph Hitler in-order-to destroy Communist Russia, which was French Grand Orient Freemasonry's creation.

After Hitler double-crossed his sponsors and made a pact with Stalin (threatening England), power swung from (English Grand Lodge Mason) Neville Chamberlain to (French Orient Mason) Winston Churchill. Nevertheless, the English branch and its Wall Street collaborators (including Prescott Bush) continued to back Hitler and later helped Nazis war criminals escape.

The phrase New World Order refers to the emergence of a one-world government. It is a conviction that has been openly acknowledged by governments and world leaders.

Some people consider the New World Order to be a scheme orchestrated by an extremely powerful and influential group: a covert fringe-Masonic organization sometimes called the "Illuminati." Various sketchy theories suggest illuminati derivations are reptilian "shape-shifters," demon worshipers, or government lackeys of aliens.

Accused of New World Order involvement is the highly secretive international think tank and influential lobbying group known as the Bilderberg Group. Also criticized is the historical Bohemian Grove secret society where some of the world's most powerful and influential men meet in a redwood forest in Monte Rio, California.

The exclusive elitists of Bohemian Grove allegedly worship a 40-foot owl statue representing the fire god Molech, and they engage in an ancient Canaanite ritual of simulated child sacrifice. This mock human sacrifice is known as "The Cremation of Care."

Rumors of child carnage began to unfold after July 13 when the dismembered body of a missing 8-year-old boy was discovered in a dumpster and in a refrigerator in the home of Brooklyn resident Levi Aron. But the worst nightmare of "Masonic child sacrifice" came to the world on July 22, with the Oslo Massacre.

Masonic "Knights Templar" Anders Breivik, a Norwegian, confessed to a shooting rampage at a liberal political youth camp on Utoya Island of Norway that took 68 young lives, after carrying out a bombing in Oslo, which killed 8.

A media press kit directly emerged containing studio photos of Anders Breivik wearing a freemason costume, with a detailed diary and a 1500 page "manifesto" describing his sect analogous to the Illuminati.

It might be a good time to point out that at least six of the skeletons in Benjamin Franklin's London home were children.

Breivik, who in the manifesto calls himself a Justiciar Knight Commander in the organization, claims that in 2008 there are anywhere from 15 to 80 others with his rank in the group in Western Europe alone. Breivik said the Knights Templar organization, heir to a famed group of Crusades-era Christian knights, was resurrected in 2002 in London by representatives from several European countries to "seize political and military control of Western European multiculturalist regimes".

The Bavarian Illuminati sect was supposedly created in the 1770s by the German banker Mayer Amschel Rothschild, who wanted to wrestle influence and power from the church in order to manipulate and control the finances of the various monarchs in Europe. Adam Weishaupt, a former Roman Catholic cleric who had developed a passionate hatred for the Jesuits, was entrusted with the cult's regulation and expansion. It was to be called the Illuminati, a Luciferian term meaning "keepers of the light."

The term Illuminati is consequently used to refer to the Rothschild bloodline families and their offshoots that make up a major portion of the controlling elite of European banking dynasties. Most members of the Illuminati are also members of major bloodlines that in many cases extend back to the 2nd century.

Emil Georg von Stauss, the president of Germany's largest bank and a major Nazi Party fundraiser, was a long-time Rothschild business associate. Some theorists hint that Adolf Hitler's grandmother, Maria Anna Schicklgruber, had sex with Baron Rothschild when she worked as a maid.

The Illuminati sacrifice children in rituals eight times a year. When Masons first join a lodge, they worship G.A.O.T.U, which they are told is the god of their own religion. When they have progressed, they are told that G.A.O.T.U. stands for the Grand Architect of the Universe. Then they search for the true name of God, which they are told was lost. In the process, they are taught that the God of the Bible is the same as the old pagan gods.

The Royal Arch Degree shows that Masons are really Baal worshipers. Most Masons do it without realizing it by participating in rituals that they really don't understand. However, a few top-level Masons (those in highest authority) know exactly what they are doing.

In Old Testament times, the Canaanites worshipped Baal by having men have sexual intercourse with temple prostitutes (both male and female, including children), and by burning babies alive. Other pagan gods were worshipped in similar ways. In some countries, this kind of pagan worship continues to this day. For example, according to eye-witness accounts, children in India are still being drowned in the Ganges River as sacrifices to pagan gods.

In the United States, the majority of Supreme Court justices were Masons from 1941 to 1971. During this time, prayer and Bible reading were prohibited in schools, and pornography was redefined to allow things that had previously been considered indecent.

Overseeing the Apollo project was Mr. Kenneth S. Kleinknecht, Manager for the Apollo Space Program.

Mr. Kleinknecht, now retired, is a 33rd degree Mason and, not coincidentally, is the brother of C. Fred Kleinknecht, the current Sovereign Grand Commander and titular head of all Scottish Rite Masons throughout the world.

NASA's space program has from the start been founded on the principles of Masonic alchemy and the magic of the mystery religions of the ancients. The prophet Daniel told us that the last day's world ruler, the antichrist king, would be mighty, *"And through his policy also he shall cause craft to prosper..." Craft, as in witchcraft!*

   Virtually everything that NASA does is permeated with magic and alchemy. Moreover, the real purpose of NASA is contained in another matrix, hidden from the public at large. This process involves the creation of Satanic ritual magic enabling the Illuminati elite to acquire and accumulate power even as the mind-controlled and manipulated masses are pushed into ever increasing states of altered consciousness.

   The truth is to know that everything is an illusion. In essence, the widely publicized successful flights and missions-and even the staggering tragedies such as the fate of the crews of the ill-fated *Challenger* and *Columbia* space shuttles-are masterfully scripted theatrical productions. It is all *Grand Theater*, hoodwink, in which some rather harmless rites are made public to deceive and charm the profane masses; while others, more sublime and evil, are concealed and known only to the elite. *Theater is, and has always been, magic.*

On February 5, 1824, Samuel Vaughan Merrick and William H. Keating founded The Franklin Institute of the State of Pennsylvania for the Promotion of the Mechanic Arts. The Franklin Institute's founding purpose was to honor Benjamin Franklin. The 191-year-old Franklin Institute Awards Program is America's oldest and most prestigious recognition of achievement in science and technology.

The Franklin Institute presents public lectures, academic symposia, and opportunities for discussion of current science events as they unfold throughout the year to create an informal and educated dialogue about the most important science issues facing the public.

The Institute is currently a lead or partner in more than a dozen federal grant-funded programs through agencies including the National Science Foundation, the National Institutes of Health, and NASA.

"We are all born ignorant, but one must work hard to remain stupid."

-Benjamin Franklin

Chapter 16   *More Than Coincidence*

The nation's space program began on March 3, 1915, or 3/3/1915; notice the date 3/3 is the same numeric representation as the number 33.

The program was called NACA, or the National Advisory Committee for Aeronautics. When congress established NACA, the following was written in the bill as the reasoning for the program: "It shall be the duty of the advisory committee for aeronautics to supervise and direct the scientific study of the problems of flight with a view to their practical solution."

The date of March 3 is extremely suspicious when you look at the significance of the number thirty-three in the history of the nation up to this point. Further, consider that in 1915, it was just one year after the institution of the Federal

Reserve and just months before the nation's entrance into World War I, which was already waging in Europe, Africa and the Middle East. In other words, the war for banking system was well underway by the time NACA was established.

March 3/ 1915 = 3+3+1+9+1+5 = 22

22 = Master Builder = Foundation

    The Freemasons are a society with a highest degree of 33, again matching that March 3 date. At the same time, Freemasons study astrology, world religions and numerology; so it is not all that big of a leap to see why they would be interested in space and space travel.

    On January 20, 1920, while President Woodrow Wilson was in office, the first President with a life number of 33, he appointed pioneering flier and aviation engineer Orville Wright to NACA's board. By the early 1920s, it had adopted a new and more ambitious mission: to promote military and civilian aviation through applied research that looked beyond current needs. NACA researchers pursued this mission through the agency's impressive collection of in-house wind tunnels, engine test stands, and flight test facilities. Commercial and military clients were also permitted to use NACA facilities on a contract basis. Thus, from the program's beginning, it was very much intertwined with the military.

Woodrow Wilson was born December 28, 1856

12/28/1856 = 1+2+2+8+1+8+5+6 = 33

12/28/56 = 12+28+56 = 96 (Freemason)

Apollo 1 was to become the first manned space mission for the lunar landing program. The shuttle was supposed to first launch on February 21, 1967, but was unable to due to a fire in the cabin during rehearsal on January 27, 1967, which killed the three participating astronauts. The numerology of the date of the fire and tragedy is quite curious.

1/27/1967 = 1+2+7+1+9+6+7 = 33

The astronauts lost were Virgil "Gus" Grissom, Edward H. White, and Roger B. Chaffee. A commemoration for the deceased crew was given on April 24, 1967.

April 24, 1967 = 4+2+4+1+9+6+7 = 33

It is sad to think that the Apollo 1 tragedy was likely a highly orchestrated event. The three astronauts who died in the tragedy were told they had been selected for the mission March 21, 1966. In the religion of Satanism, March 21, or the Spring equinox, is the most holy day of the year. It is also one day short of March 22, or 3/22, the number and date associated with Yale's Skull and Bones, another society that is infatuated with the number 33. Skull and Bones members refer to themselves as Bonesmen.

Bonesmen = 2+6+5+5+1+4+5+5 = 33

It should also be noted that the "Apollo 1" mission was first named on August 4, 1966. Interestingly enough, August 4 is President Obama's birthday, the forty-fourth President of the nation. The numerology of August 4, 1966 is interesting for two reasons.

August 4 = 8+4 = 12 = 3

1966 = 1+9+6+6 = 22

8/4/1966 = 8+4+1+9+6+6 = 34

One greater than 33...?

Thus, the date could be represented as 322. It's total sum is 34, which in the story of Dante, is a number used to reference hell or Satan. The shuttle for "Apollo 1" was first delivered to the Kennedy Space Station.

Kennedy = 2+5+5+5+5+4+7 = 33

From the numerological point of view, it is understandable why Apollo 11 landed on the moon first. 11 is a very strong number, and it has an indispensable impact on the world. Number 11 is a master number. Master number consists of 2 digits and it doubles the meaning of the corresponding single-digit number. The meaning of number 11 is assigned to leadership skills, intuition, and inspired missionaries.

Neil Armstrong is an American icon for being the first man to walk on the moon. In his career as an astronaut, he went into space twice, on two separate missions; Gemini 8 and Apollo 11. He also happens to be a man with equal name numerology the same as Thomas Jefferson.

Keep in mind the moon landing happened in the astrological time of 'Cancer'. Cancer is ruled by the moon, and its symbol is '69', like the year of the "moon landing".

Neil = 5+5+9+3 = 22 (Master = 22)

Armstrong = 1+9+4+1+2+9+6+5+7 = 44 (Space = 44) (Cancer = 44)

Neil Armstrong = 22+44 = 66 (Manifest Destiny = 66; Empire = 66)

In Neil Armstrong's Gemini 8 mission, he became the first civilian astronaut to fly into space on March 16, 1966, before returning ten-hours later, on March 17, 1966; a date with a numerology of 33.

March 17, 1966 = 3/17/1966 = 3+1+7+1+9+6+6 = 33

Gemini = 7+5+4+9+5+9 = 39

Notice the year '66, matches the name numerology of Neil Armstrong. He and David Scott also became the first astronauts to dock two ships in space. Interestingly enough, David and Neil have the same numerology.

David = 4+1+4+9+4 = 22

Neil = 5+5+9+3 = 22

Scott = 13622

Notice the coded 22

Neil's second mission into space would earn him his fame; that mission was Apollo

11, which launched at 13:32 UT, on July 16, 1969.

July 16, 1969 = 7/16/1969 =
7+1+6+1+9+6+9 = 39

For the mission, he was paired with astronauts Buzz Aldrin and Michael Collins.

Buzz = 2+3+8+8 = 21 = 3

Aldrin = 1+3+4+9+9+5 = 31

Buzz Aldrin = 3 31

Michael = 4+9+3+8+1+5+3 = 33

Collins = 3+6+3+3+9+5+1 = 30 = 3

Michael Collins = 33 3

On July 20, 1968, Neil Armstrong would land on the moon, or at least so the story goes, and utter the words, "One small step for man, one giant leap for mankind".

Neil was born August 5, 1930; a birthdate with interesting symmetry in numerology.

August 5 = 8/5 = 8+5 = 13

1930 = 1+9+3+0 = 13

Thus, 13 and 13

    Neil Armstrong would die on August 25, 2012. It was reported that the death was caused by complications to the heart. There is something curious about the date August 25 however.
8/25 = 8+25 = 33. Again, could it all be coincidence.

    It is important to keep in mind that landing on the moon, was a goal John F. Kennedy set in 1961, when he said, "before this decade is out, of landing a man on the moon, and returning him safely to earth." Neil Armstrong, Michael Collins, and Buzz Aldrin would complete that mission on July

20, and return safely to earth on July 21, 1966.

1966 was a year of foundation in numerology

1966 = 1+9+6+6 = 22, the master builder number

Kennedy = 2+5+5+5+4+7 = 33

    They especially like their 7's 11's and 33's. Remember the 33 degrees of Masonry, and that the 33rd degree praises Lucifer. Only the princes of masonry shall know the true knowledge.

    In ancient Greek mythology, every number is a letter.

    W = 6, so we will start there. So, let's compare this with the mark of the beast: 666.

www on the internet, it could have been just w. or ww. but someone chose www. = 666

The Washington Monument is 555 feet high. In inches that = 6660 inches.

Have you read House Resolution 666. Log on the Library of Congress's website and put in H.R. 666. Interesting Legislation and, also unconstitutional.

How about in the Internal Revenue Code Book: Code #666 which requires everyone to take the SS mark (social security) of course codes aren't Laws.

The universal partition code, the bar code on all the products in America, if you know the code, the first number is always 6, the middle number is always 6, and the last number is always 6 666. The company was questioned about this and they said it was a coincidence.

The new bar code in Russia to track their people is also 666.

Had the balance of power and prestige between the United States and the Soviet Union remained stable in the spring of 1961, it is quite possible that Kennedy would never have advanced his Moon program and the direction of American space efforts might have taken a radically different course. Kennedy seemed quite happy to allow NASA to execute Project Mercury at a deliberate pace, working toward the orbiting of an astronaut sometime in the middle of the decade, and to build on the satellite programs that were yielding excellent results both in terms of scientific knowledge and practical application. If Kennedy could have opted out of a big space program without hurting the country in his judgment, he would have.

Firm evidence for Kennedy's essential unwillingness to commit to an aggressive space program came in March 1961 when the NASA Administrator, James E. Webb, submitted a request that greatly expanded his agency's fiscal year 1962 budget so as to permit a Moon landing before the end of the decade. While the Apollo lunar landing program had existed as a long-term goal of NASA during the Eisenhower administration, Webb proposed greatly expanding and accelerating it. Kennedy's budget director, David E. Bell, objected to this large increase and debated Webb on the merits of an accelerated lunar landing program. In the end the president was unwilling to obligate the nation to a much bigger and more costly space program. Instead, in good political fashion, he approved a modest increase in the NASA budget to allow for development of the big launch vehicles that would eventually be required to support a Moon landing.

The masonic numerology translates into real world events. Let's compare Kennedy to Lincoln. Lincoln was elected president in 1860, Kennedy in 1960. Both were assassinated on a Friday. Lincoln was killed in Ford's Theatre; Kennedy was killed riding in a Lincoln convertible made by the Ford Motor Company. Both were succeeded by Southern Democrats named Johnson. Andrew Johnson was born in 1808, Lyndon Johnson in 1908. Andrew Johnson's name has 13 letters, Lyndon Johnson's name has 13 letters.

Lincoln was loved by the common people and hated by the establishment. So was Kennedy.

Lincoln delivered the Gettysburg Address on November 19, 1863. Kennedy was assassinated on November 22, 1963.

The first name of Lincoln's private secretary was John, the last name of Kennedy's private secretary was Lincoln. John Wilkes Booth was born in 1839, Lee Harvey Oswald in 1939. Booth shot Lincoln in a theatre and fled to a warehouse; Oswald shot Kennedy from a warehouse and fled to a theatre. John Wilkes Booth and Lee Harvey Oswald both have 15 letters. The first public suggestion that Lincoln should run for president proposed that his running mate should be John Kennedy. (John Pendleton Kennedy was a Maryland politician). Shift each letter of FBI forward by six letters in the alphabet and you get LHO, the initials of Lee Harvey Oswald.

Rathbone, who was with Lincoln when he was shot was injured. Connally was with Kennedy when he was shot and was also injured. Both Rathbone's name and Conally's name have eight letters.

Although rational explanations exist, a true believer cannot be convinced. It is in this fertile territory that number mysticism in masonic belief thrives.

The prime influences behind the American Government are Freemasons that form a host of secret societies that include the illuminati occult. The first Masonic circles began to appear around 1733 in the United States. By the time of the American Revolution, nearly 150 lodges existed throughout the colonies. American Christian Dominance initiated a delusion upon the masses for the Mason American Government to pursue its hidden agenda of the New World Order.

As a Mason goes through the 32 degrees of the Scottish rite, he surrenders his soul to the satanic occult and pursues blood sacrifice rituals. As the member progresses to the 17th degree, the Masons claim that a password will permit entrance at the judgment day to the Masonic deity, the great architect of the universe. It is said that this secret password is "Abaddon".

Revelation 9:11 They had a king over them, the angel of the Abyss, whose name in Hebrew is Abaddon, and in Greek, Apollyon".

The 'angel' of the Abyss (Hell) is really the chief demon whose name is Abaddon. Masons claim then, that the deity they worship is Abaddon!

Revelation Chapter Nine refers to the 5th angel. 5 is the occult number of death. The occult uses 9:11 as a number of destruction.

Abaddon and Apollyon both mean Destroyer.

Soon they seek a resurrection of the mythological god Apollo. In their emerging eschatology scenarios, the ancient god Apollo (a.k.a. Apollyon, Osiris or Nimrod) will resurrect from the dead, via satanic genetic tampering, and morph into the one-world dictator that the Bible calls the Antichrist. In this fanciful scenario—based solely on extra-biblical illumination, occult lore and human speculation—this "Man of Sin" will be much more than a mere man energized by Satan. He will be the king of the Nephilim (ancient "Nimrod"): part man, part devil (the literal offspring of Satan).

What's in a name? Meet Apollo. In the New Testament, the identity of the god Apollo, repeat-coded in the Great Seal of the United States as the Masonic 'Messiah' that returns to rule the earth, is the same spirit—verified by the *same name*—that will inhabit the political leader of the end-times New World Order. According to a key prophecy in the book of Second Thessalonians, the Antichrist will be the progeny or incarnation of the ancient spirit, *Apollo*. Second Thessalonians 2:3 warns: "Let no man deceive you by any means: for that day shall not come, except there come a falling away first, and that man of sin be revealed, the son of *perdition* [*Apoleia;* Apollyon, Apollo]." Numerous scholarly and classical works identify "Apollyon" as the god "Apollo"—the Greek deity "of death and pestilence," and Websters Dictionary points out that "Apollyon" was a common variant of

"Apollo" until recent history. An example of this is found in the Classical play by the ancient Greek playwright Aeschylus, *The Agamemnon of Aeschylus*, where Cassandra repeats more than once, "Apollo, thou destroyer, O Apollo, Lord of fair streets, Apollyon to me." Accordingly, the name Apollo turns up in ancient literature with the verb *apollymi* or *apollyo*, "destroy" and scholars including W.R.F. Browning believe Apostle Paul may have identified the god Apollo as the 'spirit of Antichrist' operating behind the persecuting Roman emperor, Domitian, who wanted to be recognized as 'Apollo incarnate' in his day.

Revelation 17:8 also ties the coming of Antichrist with Apollo, revealing that the 'Beast' shall ascend from the bottomless pit and enter him. "The Beast that thou sawest was, and is not; and shall ascend out of the Bottomless Pit, and go into *perdition* [*Apolia*, Apollo]: and they that dwell on the Earth shall wonder, whose names were not written in the Book of Life from the foundation of the world, when they behold the Beast that was, and is not, and yet is" (Revelation 17:8).

Abaddon is another name for Apollo (Rev. 9:11), identified historically as the king of demonic "locusts" (Revelation 9:1-11). This means among other things that Apollo is the end-times angel or "King of the Abyss" that opens the bottomless pit, out of which an army of transgenic locusts erupts upon earth.

Apollo was...and is...the great deceiver of man.

In Roman mythology, Veritas, meaning truth, was the goddess of truth. She was also the daughter of Saturn.

The Statue of Liberty, as a symbolic representation of the United States, is the image of the great harlot. In fact, Scripture foretold that a woman representing wickedness would be erected and stand upon her own pedestal in "the land of

Shinar" (Zechariah 5: 7-8, 11), a synonym for Babylon and thus the United States as the hub of the occult New World Order.

    The Statue of Liberty, the Greek and Roman goddess Libertas, is a false light and a false deity. The "New Colossus" is the name of a poem inscribed at the base of the statue. The Colossus was Helios (Apollo), also known as Mithra the sun-god and Baal or Bel of the Babylonians. As torch bearer, the Statue of Liberty is Lucifer, "the bearer of the light." This is representative of Babylon. The inhabitants of earth are "drunk with the wine of her harlotry" (Rev 17: 2).
Through her sorceries (Greek pharmakeia, the "use of, and administering of drugs") all nations are "deceived (Revelation 18: 23) and driven "mad" (Jeremiah 51: 7).

    There is a great thirst and hunger in everyone's souls looking for something that will finally satisfy them. They do not have the knowledge. They do not know what it is and they cannot explain it. But there is this soul within us that is longing for something that is genuine, and that is true. Truth is what makes us all human.

It's easy to not want to follow the breadcrumbs that are left in plain sight. It is perhaps even easier to think of those who believe in the occult as soft-minded, superstitious, new-age hippie-types who would rather commune with imaginary mystical forces than face cold, hard scientific facts. But it wasn't always so.

During the Renaissance, for example, things like Alchemy, Astrology, White Magic, Hereticism, Cabala, and Numerology were intensely studied by some of the best minds in Europe. Literature from that period is often rife with references to the occult. The works of Shakespeare are a prime example. You might even say that the study of the occult was once culturally dominant in parts of Europe. And although the occult is surely culturally marginalized as anti-scientific gobbledygook today, many historians of science believe that the study of the occult played a crucial role in the development of modern science itself. Alchemy begat chemistry and astrology begat astronomy.

During the Renaissance, students of the occult were very much in the business of trying to discover, understand and manipulate the hidden causes of everything in the universe. To that extent, their goals were very much in line with modern science.

Still, I like fairy tales. I know the idea of fairy tales can be controversial. There are those who say, "Don't teach your children about imaginary things!" And others, hardened by life's sorrows, look with disgust on the idea of fairy tales because it makes you believe in something unattainable.

But the more I face pain and disappointments in life, the more the reality of the fairy tale stands firm to me. Yes, I believe in the concept of fairy tales and they are a fact of our lives, just as much a normal part of our day as eating breakfast or putting gasoline in the car. But if I hear something that seems too good to be true, it probably is.

What we have been told, and it doesn't matter if it is from spirituality or recent discoveries in quantum and theoretical physics, our reality is actually a holographic experience (dream-like) in which we are perceiving our reality through the filters of our beliefs, judgments, and therefore spectrum for what we believe is possible.

Nikola Tesla said: "The sun is the past, the earth is the present, the moon is the future." From an incandescent mass we have originated, and into a frozen mass we shall turn. Merciless is the law of nature, and rapidly and irresistibly we are drawn to our doom.

In March, 2017 the news reported that an Israeli company had invented a vest designed to shield astronauts from deadly solar particles in deep space. They claim that the vest will protect vital human tissue, particularly stem cells, which could be devastated by solar radiation in deep space.

I would have thought that with NASA going through deep space fifty years ago, that we would have held the patent on something like that, but the patent was given to the Tel Aviv company.

In April of 2016, Christie's Auction House in London sold an end piece of a Lunar Meteorite that was found in the Sahara Desert in north west Africa for $98.366.00.

Maybe you don't have to go to the moon to get moon rocks after all.

The truth is out there. These are the words that memorably loomed against a dark sky at the end of the X-files opening credit sequence. To me, the phrase always had two meanings. The truth can be found, and the truth is very strange (as in out there). Everything and anything is available for us, *according to what we are aligning our beliefs and perceptions with*. Life has everything in it*,* every experience we could want to have is available, but we can only enjoy the things that we truly **believe** are possible. I want to believe.

"Coincidence. That's an explanation used by fools and liars."

Made in United States
Orlando, FL
04 September 2022